"So you've been warned against me?"

Antonio asked the question harshly. "You think I've been trying to seduce you for your share of Tradaro's?" he went on. "Who else fits your insinuation, Francesca? What other man on the island has had the opportunity, the insolence, to kiss you as I did?"

"No one!" Half indignant, she looked up at him, green eyes bright. Anger stirred but the softness of appeal still lingered. "Tonio, you don't—"

"Go away and leave me in peace!" he said fiercely.

"If you mean will I leave you in sole possession of Tradaro's—never!" she declared breathlessly. "The only way you'll get my half is by marrying me, as Andres said. And that isn't even a possibility!"

Antonio swore in Spanish. "I would as soon be married to a *regañona* — a shrew!"

Trader's Cay

by

REBECCA STRATTON

Harlequin Books

TORONTO • LONDON • LOS ANGELES • AMSTERDAM
SYDNEY • HAMBURG • PARIS • STOCKHOLM • ATHENS • TOKYO

Original hardcover edition published in 1980
by Mills & Boon Limited

ISBN 0-373-02376-6

Harlequin edition published December 1980

CHAPTER ONE

To Francesca the name Trader's Cay was one she had heard for the first time less than a year before, but it had conjured up all sorts of exotic dreams during the ensuing months. Palm trees, sandy beaches, moonlight nights and barbecues on the beach; a life of glorious ease and pleasure provided for by the thriving estate left to her by her grandfather. Now all those months of eager anticipation were about to culminate in breathless reality, and she followed the direction of the pointing finger with fluttering excitement and not a little apprehension.

'Straight ahead,' the man beside her said, and glanced at her sideways from narrow dark eyes set in a well-weathered face. 'Tain't very big, you see?'

'It doesn't look very big,' Francesca conceded cautiously.

In fact she had no idea just how large Trader's Cay ought to look at that distance. She felt it looked larger than she expected somehow, although the heat haze made it shimmer deceptively, but she could make out the unmistakable feather-mop shapes of coconut palms, and that in itself was exciting, and confirmed one aspect of her dreams.

'You family?' the skipper of the schooner asked, and it was clear that both her identity and her reason for visiting the island intrigued him.

He was a small man, dark-skinned and friendly and his accent was the lilting sing-song English of the Jamaican, for it was in Jamaica that Francesca's flight from London had put down. His schooner plied the island routes like so many others, but he alone had been prepared to take her to Trader's Cay. Off the regular routes, some said, but this

man called there regularly and was therefore a possible
source of information as far as Francesca was concerned.

'I'm no relation,' she told him, assuming he referred to the
current resident of the island. 'Do you know Mr Morales
personally, captain?'

'Seen him plenty a times, an' dealt with him,' the
captain informed her readily. 'But he ain't a man you gets to
know, missie, you got me? Spanish family, like mos' of 'em
round here—island Spanish. They owned the Cay since——'

His shrug confined the Morales' ownership of the Cay to
infinity, but it was a misconception Francesca hastened to
amend. 'My grandfather owned it for nearly thirty years
before he died early this year,' she told him. 'Mr Francis
Dale; did you know him?'

'See him a couple a times,' the captain said. 'Don' know
nuthin' 'bout him ownin' the Cay, though.'

Quite clearly he was unconvinced, but Francesca was not
inclined to press the matter for the moment, there was too
much else to claim her attention. She watched, fascinated,
as the deep blue Caribbean cleft before the schooner's bow
and folded back in a white lacy vee as the wind sent the
vessel racing before it towards the island. It was an exciting
way to travel anywhere, and knowing that she was on the
way to lay claim to a half-share in a tropical island added to
the enjoyment. Even so, she admitted to feeling a growing
nervousness as well, the nearer they got to their destination.

Francesca had seen nothing and heard little of her grandfather, Francis Dale, and yet it was through him that she
had embarked on this venture into an entirely new world.
Francis Dale had taken off abroad when he was widowed,
and for some time had virtually disappeared; then, shortly
before Francesca was born, her father had heard from him.
Far from being lonely and destitute, as was feared, he was
the owner of property and a quite wealthy man, growing
bananas and citrus fruit in the Caribbean.

For the next sixteen years father and son had corresponded, very intermittently, exchanging only the most superficial news of their respective health and well-being. From the little her father had passed on to her Francesca had learned that her grandfather had bought the estate of a widow who was unable to cope with running it and at the same time raise a son, too young to be of help. It was only later, after her father died and her mother remarried, that Francesca gleaned certain other facts concerning her adventurous grandparent.

The letters had ceased altogether when her father died, and her mother had discouraged any interest in the man she had never regarded as anything more than a reprobate adventurer, however well he had done in his new life. Bit by bit, however, Francesca had gathered the information that the widow who originally owned the estate had stayed on in the house. As the old man's mistress, so her mother claimed, although what grounds she had for such an assumption, Francesca never discovered. Presumably the arrangement had been an amicable one, conventional or not, because the woman's son still lived there and was in fact the man she was on her way to meet.

Francesca was twenty-two when events occurred that were likely to change her whole life. It seemed that during the last few months of his life Francis Dale remembered the granddaughter he had never seen and, with an impulsive gesture that she could well believe was typical of him, had made her co-heir to his estate, along with Antonio Morales, the widow's son. So, with only the bare bones of the situation to guide her, and against her mother's rather acid advice, Francesca had decided to go out and stake her claim personally, with no idea what kind of reception she was likely to get.

Presumably the estate was being run in the meantime by Antonio Morales, but such practical matters were beyond her scope, and she was far more inclined to dwell on the prospect of an idyllic life, far removed from the mundane routine of a London office. The schooner captain had confirmed that Antonio Morales was Spanish-Creole, but she wondered if he spoke any English at all, or if her grandfather had learned to speak a new language during his thirty years of self-imposed exile. Nor did she know whether or not the widow was still alive, for she was likely to be her grandfather's age, in which case the son was probably a man about forty or so.

'Did you say the ole man livin' with M's Morales was your gran-pappy?' the captain asked, and Francesca instinctively resented his bland and unselfconcious use of the term 'living with'.

'My grandfather bought Trader's Cay from her nearly thirty years ago, when he first came out from England,' she told him. 'I believe it was just after her husband died.'

'We-e-ell, man!' Obviously her grandfather's ownership had been a well-kept secret, although Francesca could not imagine why. 'I never know he owned the Cay; bet there ain't many folks do!' He chuckled gleefully as if he anticipated being the one to spread the news. 'Mr Morales run that place the last twelve-fifteen year, an' it seemed like he just took over natural-like when he come of age. Ain't nobody know he ain't the boss, I bet!'

'He is now,' Francesca informed him. 'At least he's half-owner; my grandfather left it to us jointly.'

'That right?' Again a slightly malicious chuckle anticipated the future relish to be had from relating the information, straight from the horse's mouth as it were. 'I bet M'st Morales don' take kindly to that!'

Francesca took her eyes off the palm-fringed island for a moment and eyed him curiously. Any information about Antonio Morales, she felt, would put her slightly less at a disadvantage, and however superficial the captain's knowledge of the man, he obviously must know something about him. 'What is he like, captain?' she asked, turning her face in to the cooling breeze; and hurried on to counter any misunderstanding, 'Is he a friendly man?'

Once more the man's sharp dark eyes quizzed her profile for a second before he answered, and it was possible he sensed her nervousness and sympathised. 'I wouldn't say friendly exactly, missie,' he told her, then broke off to yell something unintelligible to the man at the wheel. He must have noticed her expression as he turned back, for he was shaking his head and his smile had the eternal optimism of the islander. 'Ain't no call to worry,' he assured her cheerfully. 'He ain't a bad man, an' he's honest an' straight-dealin' even though he don' bear no nonsense. That young 'un, now——'

'Young one?' Francesca took him up swiftly, but the captain took his time enlightening her.

Rocking forward on his toes, he peered down into the water, then up at the main mast and the sail bellying in the brisk wind. His gnarled mahogany hands gripped the bow rail while he took critical note of their gradual change of direction and he yelled more instructions to the helmsman. The schooner dipped obediently to port as it tacked into a crosswind, and Francesca waited until the manoeuvre was completed to his satisfaction before prompting him.

'Who were you talking about, captain?' she asked, and he once more gave her his attention.

'He called Andrés Morales.' His inexpert pronunciation made the first name unrecognisable, but it was clear he expected her to be better informed. 'He M'st Morales' son, missie, an' I heard tell he's a *wild* one! He come back here last spring from his schoolin', jus' 'fore the ole man die.' He eyed her curiously. 'You don' know 'bout him?'

'I didn't,' Francesca confessed, and mused on who else she could expect to find living on her island.

For the moment she was to continue in ignorance regarding Antonio Morales' son, for the captain's presence was needed elsewhere, and he left her standing alone at the bow rail, watching Trader's Cay become a solid reality before her eyes. It seemed to grow rapidly once they were on their new course, and the palm trees became more than simply a feathery promise on the skyline.

Her heart began to hammer urgently as the schooner swept by the white-sanded shore in deep blue water and made for a sturdy wooden pier where its arrival was a signal for men, women and children to come running from all directions. Cheerfully grinning and chattering in a chaotic mixture of broken English and Spanish, willing hands made fast the mooring lines as the schooner slid smoothly alongside the pier.

There was little at that point to suggest the island paradise Francesca had dreamed of so often in the past months, for the palm trees were obscured by a row of enormous sheds that were built facing the pier and accessible from it by an apron of concrete on which vast piles of crates were stacked. Over to one side, a pair of stringy mules hitched to a cart stood dozing patiently in the sun, while a small boy rested his back against one of the cart wheels, his bare scrawny knees jack-knifed under his chin as he watched the general activity with a faintly bored expression.

The heat was intense away from the freshening ocean wind, and already Francesca felt sticky and hot, and very uncomfortable in her linen dress and jacket, and dreamed longingly of lounging in the shade on her very own beach. The schooner was not simply there to bring her, she realised as she watched the cheerful chaos on shore with mixed feelings. It also brought mail and supplies, and provided a brief but welcome change of company for the island people. It all looked very friendly and happy down there, but Francesca felt horribly out of her depth as she stood there, and she welcomed the sudden reappearance of the captain with an inward sigh of relief, for she had no idea what she ought to do next.

'Come on, missie,' he told her cheerfully, and handed her down the narrow gangway with commendable gallantry, while one of his crew carried her cases. 'M'st Morales be here soon; he don' let nobody put in without he come to see for hisself.'

'Thank you, captain.'

'You welcome!'

He touched the peak of his cap, grinned encouragingly and left her once more, standing on the concrete apron and looking about her in obvious indecision. Her first close sight of her island wasn't quite what she expected, but she clung hopefully to the recollection of palm trees and a white-sanded beach. This was obviously the more practical aspect of the estate, and she must not judge hastily, or on such short acquaintance.

She felt very isolated alone on that expanse of scorching hot concrete. Her copper red hair gleamed like fire in the sun and her pale skin was flushed with the heat and with the sudden onset of actual panic when she realised that with the departure of the schooner would go her contact with the outside world for heaven knew how long. Maybe Antonio Morales was not going to put in an appearance on this occasion. Maybe he would make his non-appearance a kind of gesture that would leave her in little doubt of his feelings. The schooner captain had anticipated his dislike of having to share his inheritance.

'Ah, Miss Dale!' Francesca turned quickly to find the blazing heat lessened slightly by a tall shadow that enabled her to get a clear sight of the man who made it. 'I am Antonio Morales.'

No mention of welcoming her, Francesca noticed as she took the extended hand, and she just managed not to wince when her fingers were crushed by a brief but powerful grasp. Hastily pulling herself together, she murmured a conventional greeting. 'How do you do, Mr Morales?'

Her throat felt horribly parched and her voice sounded husky and not quite steady. She could not be making a very good first impression, she felt, but he had taken her unawares and put her at a disadvantage. Taking surreptitious stock of the man she had come so far to see, she was not quite sure how he struck her in those first few seconds.

He was taller than she expected, and younger, although he would be in his late thirties, she guessed. Dark, as she expected knowing his name and his ancestry, but he had eyes that were a bright deep blue and so unexpected in that very Spanish face that Francesca frankly stared for several seconds before recovering herself. He was not handsome, but he was very definitely attractive and stunningly masculine in a way that immediately appealed to her very feminine senses.

A cream shirt, staggeringly effective with a mahogany dark tan, showed a long vee of brown throat and fitted closely across a broad chest. Fawn trousers, the bottoms tucked into short boots, closely followed the lean, rangy lines of his body and long legs, arrogantly and uninhibitedly masculine. Whatever Trader's Cay lacked in the way of amenities, Antonio Morales obviously had access to the services of an excellent tailor.

'I have the *carruaje* here to take you to the house, if you will come with me, Miss Dale.' He spoke excellent English with only a trace of accent, and Francesca once more brought herself swiftly back to earth, glancing automatically over her shoulder to where her three suitcases stood near the foot of the gangway. He noticed the half-anxious gesture and responded immediately. 'Jose will take care of your baggage; please come with me.'

He sounded vaguely impatient, so that Francesca hastened

to do as he said, and as she walked across the concrete with that tall and slightly forbidding figure beside her she was aware of being watched by almost every pair of eyes within sight. Under the shadow of a cluster of palm trees behind the sheds stood an old-fashioned horse-drawn carriage with a glossy chestnut mare between the shafts, and an elderly Negro perched up on the driver's seat.

The man jumped down as they approached, and touched his forehead with bunched fingers when Antonio Morales spoke to him, so that for a moment Francesca began to wonder if she had been transported to another time as well as to another world. Presumably the driver had been despatched to fetch her suitcases, for he scuttled off at once, leaving his employer to assist her into the vehicle. Such quaint luxury was completely unexpected and delighted her so much that she smiled to herself as she accepted the assistance of one large brown hand under her arm and grasping her elbow.

There was a roof to keep off the sun, but the sides and front were open and the interior was upholstered in red velvet. The well-sprung chassis swayed a little as she took her seat and she spread her hands either side of her, savouring the pleasantly unexpected, and leaving her reaction in little doubt.

'This is wonderful,' she declared impulsively. 'I didn't expect anything like this!'

Antonio Morales stood with a hand either side of the opening and regarded her for a moment with those disturbing blue eyes and, she noticed, with not so much as a glimmer of a smile as yet. 'There are no motor vehicles on the island,' he informed her. 'The carriage belongs to my mother, but she wishes you to use it whenever you wish.'

'That's very good of her, and I'll certainly use it sometimes.' Her green eyes showed just how delighted she was with what could only be a gesture of welcome surely.

Obviously the widow was still alive, and it was a relief, somehow, to know it, for her son had made no move to suggest he welcomed her as yet. 'I must thank her the moment I arrive.'

A mere inclination of his head acknowledged her thanks, then he stepped back quickly when the driver returned carrying one case himself, and followed by a boy carrying the other two. 'This is all you have?'

Somehow he managed to convey a touch of derision, and Francesca felt a flush of colour in her already warm cheeks. 'In the world!' she agreed with deliberate facetiousness. 'Except for a half-share in Trader's Cay, of course.'

That had been irresistible, and Francesca saw the sudden tightening of his lips, guessing that those broodingly dark looks concealed a temper. 'My mother is waiting for you at the house,' he told her. 'I shall follow in a few moments, but Jose will deliver you safely. *Adiós*, Miss Dale.'

The driver clucked encouragingly and flicked the reins, and so began their sedate drive along a dusty and half-made road towards what to Francesca looked like a veritable forest of massive ragged leaves sprayed like huge fans against a blue sky. 'Are these bananas?' she asked, leaning forward in her seat and addressing the stooped back; but the answer became obvious even before the man turned his head and looked at her for a moment with a puzzled frown, until she pointed to the green fruit.

Then he nodded his grizzled head and showed broken and stained teeth in a smile. 'Ah, *sí, señorita—los plátanos*.'

Clearly the man spoke little or no English, so Francesca made no further attempt to converse, but looked around her instead; after all, this seemingly endless plantation was half hers. The overshadowing banana leaves did, in fact, eventually come to an end and they were driving across an expanse of surprisingly lush grass.

Once more Francesca's heart began its urgent thudding

beat, for not too far distant she caught a glimpse of a roof-top, showing through a screen of flowering shrubs and huge trees. A row of white-painted outbuildings stood half hidden to the right of it, and beyond, row upon row of what she took to be citrus trees. It was hard to realise when she looked around that they were so near to the sea, and that white-sanded beach she had so often anticipated with pleasure, and she felt wildly excited.

It was a moment or two before she realised that someone was riding out to meet them, and her own feeling of pleasant anticipation was only a little subdued by the suspicion that the words the old driver muttered in Spanish were very likely curses. The rider, whoever he was, came at breakneck speed on an animal that looked as if it had been bred for the racecourse, and as he came closer, something about him made Francesca tighten her hold on her handbag and moisten her lips uneasily.

'Who is it?' She leaned forward and tugged at the driver's coat as she asked the question, and the old man shook his head, his hold on the reins tightening perceptibly.

'Señor Andrés, *señorita*,' he said, and eyed the newcomer with obvious anxiety, so that Francesca's uneasiness increased.

'He's——'

A shrill yell cut her short and startled the high-bred mare between the shafts into tossing her head nervously. The old Negro murmured to the mare softly in Spanish and tried to soothe her, at the same time watching the rider come nearer and nearer. The young man did not attempt to slow down at all, but came on, yelling wildly and whipping his mount to greater effort as he leaned forward along the animal's glossy neck and wielded a long Spanish quirt with ruthless energy.

In other circumstances it might have been possible to admire his skill as a horseman, but it was no time for admiring a stupidly dangerous manoeuvre, however skilled. He rode directly across the path of the carriage, swerving at the very last moment, and the mare whinnied in fright, only the reassuring words of her driver making her go on, while Francesca clung to the side of the carriage and held her breath.

Turning his mount, the rider came back, yelling still and using his heels as well as the quirt to spur the animal to greater effort, bent it seemed on frightening the mare out of control. Though for what purpose was beyond Francesca, and she hung on grimly, her anger growing in company with an undeniable fear.

'Señor Andrés!'

Beyond that one plea the old Negro could do nothing but try to control the panicking mare as she screamed and shook her head wildly, terrified both by the wild yells of the rider and the too close proximity of the horse he rode. Again they turned and rode directly across the path of the carriage, the horse's hooves pounding into the dusty ground like a drum beat, and once more making a last-minute swerve almost under the nose of the panic-stricken mare.

It was too much for the mare; wild-eyed and sweating, she snatched control from the frightened old man and took to her heels in an attempt to outrun her tormentor. Her head back, she flew for home with her mane streaming in the wind and her nostrils flared, while the carriage rocked and swayed alarmingly. It was in imminent danger of turning over, but Francesca felt more anger than fear now, and while she clung to the side of the runaway carriage she managed to see the face of the rider, her green eyes glittering angrily.

Having achieved his object, he rode alongside for a moment or two to enjoy the result, and she had the opportunity to get a look at Antonio Morales' son. He was young, no more than seventeen or eighteen, she guessed, and handsome in a youthful and immature way, with bright dark eyes and a full-lipped mouth that smiled as much in mockery as amusement. He kept pace with the carriage without for a moment attempting to do anything about bringing it to a halt, and her feellngs showed clearly on Francesca's pale face.

Whatever she had expected by way of a response it was not the sudden yell of laughter he gave just before he turned his mount and veered off across the open ground towards the citrus groves. Possibly he had seen what Francesca was as yet unaware of, or perhaps his departure was mere coincidence, but while she watched him ride away and clung grimly to the side of the swaying carriage, another rider came up beside them, riding out of nowhere, it seemed.

Antonio Morales rode every bit as well as his son did, but with more control and less dangerous bravado. His face was grim and his mouth set hard as he passed Francesca in the carriage without so much as a glance, racing his mount towards the already tiring mare. She saw him lean out and snatch the curb strap, forcing his will on the terrified animal until she yielded finally and slid to a halt with her haunches almost on the ground.

The glossy hide was foam-flecked and the huge eyes rolling in fear, but the man checked her and somehow managed to dismount while still retaining his hold. Standing by the straining neck, he soothed big hands over her and murmured in Spanish, as if to a frightened child. The welfare of the animal, it seemed, was of more importance to him than that of his guest, and Francesca stepped down from the carriage unassisted, then stood for a moment on legs that felt scarcely able to support her.

Her face was without colour and her green eyes looked huge and luminously bright against the pallor of her skin. She was shaken, but she was angry too, and determined to let Antonio Morales know what she thought of his son's dangerous and vicious behaviour. She had no doubt that it had been meant to convey his personal feelings, but she had no intention of being driven away from her own property by anyone, no matter how he felt about her being there.

'I don't know what that idiot thought he was doing,' she said in a decidedly unsteady voice, 'but he should be locked up as a dangerous lunatic!'

The mare had settled down and although she was still trembling she was docile enough when Antonio Morales turned from her and looked at Francesca, something in his eyes making a shiver along her spine. 'My son is not insane, Miss Dale,' he said in his impeccable English, and his voice was as chill as ice. 'He feels strongly about Tradaro's, and he has not the maturity or the control to keep those feelings to himself.'

Vaguely Francesca noticed something different about the name he used, but for the moment she was more concerned with his excuses for his son's abominable behaviour. 'I presume you mean that he thinks I have no right to be here, Mr Morales,' she guessed, and there was a stubborn lift to her chin as she faced him. 'But as I see it, I have more right to be resentful than either of you. It was *my* grandfather who owned this place for the past thirty years, and——'

'And it is *I* who have worked it for the past fifteen of those years, Miss Dale, or else there would have been no estate for you to inherit!' The clipped precise English cut her short, and Francesca was wary enough of him to take heed of the look in his eyes when he said it. Moving from the mare's bowed head, he stood waiting beside her, obviously ready to help her into the carriage again and the proffered hand, when she accepted it, bound strong, steely fingers over hers and gripped them bruisingly hard. 'You may continue quite safely now, and I shall ride with you to ensure that there is no mishap, you need have no fear.'

'I'm not frightened,' Francesca denied swiftly and unhesitatingly, 'I'm angry! I don't frighten easily, Mr

Morales, and I hope you'll tell your son that!'

Curiously enough she could detect no anger in those strangely anomalous blue eyes, only a kind of curiosity. But still he did not smile, only inclined his head gravely as if acknowledging her right to be angry, then stepped back and signalled the driver to go on. It was quite instinctive to glance from the corner of her eyes when he remounted and took up a position just slightly ahead of where she sat, and she felt vaguely annoyed because her heart fluttered unexpectedly at the sight of his tall, straight figure keeping guard on them.

The house was reached in just a few moments, and the carriage swept around a graceful curved driveway, encircling a very formal flower bed that had a huge stone basin set in the very centre of it. A white marble figure, smoothed by the years to an unrecognisable tangle of feminine anatomy, held a horn of plenty from which water spouted into the basin and the tinkling sound of it seemed blessedly cool as the carriage drew up in front of an imposing façade.

The style was, not unexpectedly, colonial Spanish, elegantly faced with rounded arches and slender supporting pillars. The upper storey projected over the lower, and the balconies were fronted by ornamental grilles and draped with vines of purple and pink, and windows like huge dark eyes peered from between yet more vines. Two enormous immortelles soared upward behind the house, and a riot of red hibiscus frothed about its lower half and hid a good half of it from view.

While she sat admiring it, Antonio Morales handed his horse over to a man who appeared to have been waiting to perform just that task for him. A hand indicated that she should accompany him across a blue-tiled porch formed by the upper floor, and she glanced sideways at him as he walked beside her to the open door. Her immediate reaction was to shiver in the sudden chill coolness when she stepped out of the heat of the sun, and he turned and looked at her curiously.

So far he had not asked how she felt after the near-disaster caused by his son, and in her heart Francesca resented his apparent unconcern. At the same time, she told herself she must be on her guard where Andrés Morales was concerned, for he was obviously not only hostile but downright dangerous, and it was just possible he had his father's approval.

'You suffered nothing more than fright, Miss Dale?'

The question was asked as they stepped from the porch into a wide cool hall tiled in the same blue as the porch outside, and as he asked he turned and made an oddly disturbing survey of her inch by inch until Francesca felt herself colouring furiously. It also gave the impression that he was seeing her for the first time, and made her feel more uneasy than ever, but she vowed not to underplay the incident, whatever his opinion.

'I'm bruised from being thrown about,' she told him, 'and I was lucky not to be thrown out of the carriage.' She looked up into that dark and very Spanish face and met his eyes determinedly. 'I hope you don't expect me to simply take it sitting down, Mr Morales, because I don't intend to! However you feel about it, it was a stupid and dangerous stunt to pull, and somebody should tell him so! If you don't——'

'I shall deal with my son in my own way, Miss Dale!'

The blue eyes darkened with warning and once again Francesca yielded when she should perhaps have been more insistent. But Antonio Morales was not an easy man to outface, and it was obvious he would not countenance her being the one to reprimand his son, whatever her rights as the chief victim of his malice.

She did, however, give him a look which fairly conveyed her belief that, if he had not condoned his son's behaviour, he at least sympathised with his motives. And the meaning of it was not lost, as she soon discovered. They came to a halt in the centre of the hall and he turned to face her, his mouth set hard and firm into a straight line below an arrogantly haughty nose.

'I believe it is said in your country, Miss Dale, that people with red hair are hot-tempered, but I would not advise you to lose your temper with Andrés over this incident or I fear you will be the loser.'

Her heart rapping urgently, Francesca faced him, her colour high and a warning light deep in her green eyes. 'I'm not in the habit of being nice to people who try and scare me to death, Mr Morales, whatever you do in your country! When I see Andrés again I can't guarantee that I won't tell him exactly what I think of him, and in no uncertain terms!'

For a second she could have sworn that both surprise and a hint of humour showed in the gaze that fixed so steadily on her flushed face. But if it was ever there it quickly vanished and left him looking as stern and uncompromising as ever. 'To all intents this is Morales country, Miss Dale; not England or Spain, but Morales country. Here we make our own rules, most of which are designed for our benefit, and allow us to behave as we will on our own territory, so do not expect to be welcomed as warmly as if you were an invited guest.'

Francesca's cheeks burned, her eyes blazing furiously as she stood, trembling, in the middle of that big cool hall. Her instinct was to hit out; to strike that arrogantly confident face as hard as she could, but with almost superhuman restraint, she resisted it. Brawling with him was not the way to start, nor the way to impress him with her suitability as a landowner.

'For the last thirty years,' she reminded him in a thin strained voice that shook more than she hoped, 'this has been Dale property, Mr Morales. Whatever reason your mother had for selling it, she let it go to my grandfather and you lost your right to it! The fact that my grandfather left it to you *and* me shows that he did not intend to yield it entirely to the Morales again, no matter how right they feel their claim is! This is Morales and Dale territory, Mr Morales, and I mean share and share alike!'

Try as she would, Francesca could not stop her gaze from straying to the big brown hands that gripped the quirt they carried as if he was set to use it, and she shivered. He was angry, how could he not be? But he was much more controlled than his son and the fury he felt burned deep in his blue eyes but was not allowed to break out.

'I will see to it that you take an active and equal part in the running of Tradaro's,' he told her in a deep, firm voice. 'But remember, *señorita*, that the decision was yours! Please — —' He extended a hand, indicating a door that led off the hall, the middle one of three. 'My mother is waiting to meet you.'

Still shaking from the fury of the exchange, Francesca obeyed his unspoken command and walked on while he fell into step just half a pace behind her, adding to her discomfiture by being visible only if she kept glancing over her shoulder. He opened the door, then stood back to allow her into the room first, looking down his nose at her as she passed him.

It was the most attractive room Francesca had ever seen. The furniture was heavy and dark and highly polished with a patina of age to enhance its glowing richness. Francesca remembered one holiday staying in a very old house in Spain that had been turned into an hotel but still retained its original character, and this room reminded her of it.

Even the woman who stood over near the window at the far end of the room seemed to fit exactly into the picture of well-to-do comfort and elegance, and Antonio Morales went across to her, then half-turned to Francesca, as if to summon her to them. 'Madre, this is Miss Dale; Miss Dale, my mother, Señora Cecilia Morales.'

She was a tall woman, running to plumpness, and her hair was almost completely grey with only touches of its original black still lingering above a fine broad brow. Her eyes were dark and were still quite beautiful for all they were fading a little with age, and she carried herself as gracefully as a young girl, her head high and with no hint of stoop on her shoulders, her arms covered by the long sleeves of a fawn silk dress.

Most important of all, she was smiling, and it was the first genuine sign of welcome that Francesca had received, so that she expanded warmly in its generosity. 'Miss Dale!' Plump fingers clasped hers eagerly and she was subjected to a scrutiny both keen and friendly. 'You are most welcome to Tradaro's.'

Not entirely, Francesca knew, but she accepted that her hostess's welcome was genuine enough and smiled. 'Thank you, Mrs—Señora——'

'Señora Morales, Miss Dale,' Antonio Morales' deep, smooth voice informed her. 'We are Spanish and have always been so.'

'Not always so, Tonio,' his mother corrected him, and her eyes sparkled with mischief, as if she knew he did not like being reminded. 'My grandfather was a Welsh sea captain, Miss Dale, which will explain to you why my son has his blue eyes.'

It was automatic to look at the eyes in question, but Francesca found them fixed rather disconcertingly on her, and hastily looked away again. 'I hadn't noticed,' she murmured, and noticed the faint smile of disbelief on Cecilia Morales' face. Hastening to cover her embarrassment, she went on to another matter, one that had puzzled her earlier. 'I've noticed that both you and Mr Morales refer to this island as something different; I've only heard it called Trader's Cay.'

'An old mistake,' Antonio Morales informed her before his mother could enlighten her. 'The island was originally the property of a Spanish seaman called Tradaro, more than three hundred years ago. It was then called simply Tradaro's, the Cay was added some time later. When Alonso Morales bought it in 1687, his coming led to the misnomer it now has. He was a merchant; to the English, a trader, and it was an easy transition from Tradaro's Cay as it had been to Trader's Cay, as it now is to most people.'

'But not to you!'

She caught and held his eyes for just a moment and the contact again brought a curious shivering sensation to her too responsive senses, a sensation that ceased abruptly when the door opened with a kind of flourish and Andrés Morales came in. He stood for a moment in the doorway, as if he was in two minds whether or not to come in, then he smiled and came striding across the room, encircling his grandmother's shoulders with an arm while he stared quite deliberately at Francesca.

'*Señorita!*' His slight bow and the gleaming brightness in his eyes mocked her, and Francesca felt herself flushing warmly when she recalled his behaviour earlier.

Cecilia Morales looked vaguely puzzled when her son frowned so blackly, but it was clear that she adored her grandson, and taken purely at face value Andrés Morales was a handsome and very attractive young man. As long as one did not look too closely at that gleam of malice in his eyes and the thin, cruel line of his mouth.

'Andrés,' his grandmother said, 'this is Miss Dale——'

'I know,' Andrés informed her, unabashed by his father's black frown. 'You look no worse for your—experience, *señorita.*'

Furious at his matter-of-fact attitude, Francesca glared at

him, but the retort that sprang to her lips was never allowed to materialise, for Antonio Morales took firm control of the situation. 'You will come with me,' he told his son in firm, deliberate English. 'I wish to examine the horse you were riding.'

For just a moment the younger man looked very much a schoolboy and without knowing quite why, Francesca even felt a qualm of sympathy for him. But he had driven his mount cruelly hard, and Antonio Morales had shown how much he cared for his horses when he handled the frightened mare. No one would have dared question him at that moment, Francesca thought, except his mother, and Cecilia was looking from one to the other curiously.

'Come!' Antonio ordered, and went striding towards the door, not doubting for a moment that his son would follow.

For a full minute neither of the women spoke, then Mrs Morales looked at Francesca and shook her head, an uncertain smile trembling on her lips. 'I do not understand what they are about,' she confessed, 'but I must apologise for neglecting you, Miss Dale. If you will come with me I will show you to your room myself.' She glanced at Francesca from the corner of her eye as they crossed the room together. 'Perhaps you will enlighten me about what has made my son so angry and Andrés so wary of him.'

It wasn't a task Francesca relished, but as they crossed the hall and mounted a wide, polished stairway to the upper floor, she recounted the incident of the runaway carriage as briefly as possible, but put the blame firmly where it belonged. It was clear that as she listened Cecilia Morales disliked what she heard, and when Francesca finished telling it she shook her head.

'If Andrés rode his animal as hard as you say——'

'He rode like a fury,' Francesca insisted, seeing no reason to spare her tormentor. 'The poor animal had no choice but to go as fast as he could with that horrible whip driving him all the time.'

'And Tonio will see it,' said Cecilia Morales, half to herself, Francesca thought. 'Oh, *Dios*!'

Puzzled, Francesca looked at her enquiringly. '*Señora*——'

Cecilia Morales held her hands together in front of her and smiled, but it was a smile that did not reach her eyes, and Francesca noticed it. 'I am sorry, Miss Dale, but I am a little—concerned. You see, this has happened before; that Andrés had ridden one of the horses, as your grandfather used to say, into the ground. He was a kindly man, *mi querido* Francisco, but he did not expect Tonio to take the same view, not where an animal was concerned. Tonio threatened that if ever Andrés treated one of the horses so badly again he would——' She bit her lip anxiously and was shaking her head. 'Oh, but I wish Andrés would take more care!'

A suspicion rose and was subdued again hastily, and Francesca looked at the older woman and frowned. 'He told me he would deal with his son in his own way, Señora Morales; what exactly did he mean?'

'He warned Andrés that if he ill-used one of the horses like that again——' She shook her head, trying to convince herself. 'He warned Andrés that he would deal with him in the same way as he did the horse.'

'Oh, but he *wouldn't*!'

Francesca made the claim hastily and without knowledge of the man in question, but a look at Cecilia Morales' face almost convinced her how wrong she was. The older woman's fading dark eyes were anxious as she leaned forward and opened a bedroom door. 'You do not know my son,' she said, and Francesca frowned at her uneasily.

'I'm not sure I want to!' she declared, and felt sure she meant it.

CHAPTER TWO

It was the two huge immortelle trees growing quite near to Francesca's bedroom window that brought home to her just how much of what she had imagined about Trader's Cay was actual fact. The big untidy trees with their exotic red blooms were just the kind of thing she had anticipated, and they, along with all the other colourful and fragrant trees and shrubs, were enough so far to convince her that she had done the right thing in coming out to the Caribbean personally to claim her inheritance.

There would be drawbacks, she did not doubt it having met Antonio Morales and his son, but she had liked Cecilia Morales and thought she was liked in turn. Dinner the night before had been rather an ordeal, but she had been glad to go to bed early and catch up on some of the sleep she had missed lately.

Drifting off to sleep with the exotic and heady scents from the garden soothing her tiredness, Francesca promised herself a more relaxed day in the morning. She would find herself a small beach like the one she had noticed on the way in, and simply laze for a few hours, then she would explore a little, and from then on take things as they came. Her own Caribbean island was something she had looked forward to, something she meant to enjoy, and she was smiling to herself as she drifted off to sleep.

She stirred uneasily from a deep sleep, what seemed like only minutes later, when a loud and insistent knocking invaded the dream she was having. Burying her head, she tried to shut it out, but it started up again after only a few seconds and reluctantly she rolled over and glared at the bedroom door with drooping eyes, kept awake by the knocking on the thick wood panels.

Rubbing sleep from her eyes, she glanced at the window and realised it was daylight, though not the full blazing daylight of yesterday. 'I'm coming!' She slipped her feet into slippers and her arms into a robe which she pulled on as she walked across the room, yawning and shaking herself awake. 'I'm *coming*!'

The last was in response to a further knock, and she felt not a little irritated to think that not even now she was no longer a working girl was she allowed to sleep on in the morning. Her red hair was tousled and sleep still lay heavy on her eyelids when she opened the door, and her annoyance showed plainly in drawn brows, but she snatched at the neck of the robe when she found Antonio Morales standing outside her door.

He was dressed more or less as he had been yesterday, when she first saw him, except that this morning a snowy white shirt did even more for that stunningly dark tan. He stood directly facing her with his feet planted firmly apart on the landing carpet and he was regarding her sleepy face with an intensity that Francesca found infinitely disturbing.

'Good morning, Miss Dale.'

Francesca blinked, hastily dragging herself to consciousness, and shook her head dazedly. 'G-good morning.' Clutching the robe more tightly, she felt the colour rise in her cheeks when his gaze moved from her face down over the slender figure that was rather too clearly defined by the clingingly soft robe. 'I don't understand what——'

'I see you are not yet dressed,' he interrupted shortly. 'Will you please be as quick as you can, Miss Dale, there is much to be done this morning with a green boat coming in.' He noted her complete blankness and explained brusquely, 'A boat coming to collect the green fruit for transport to the U.K., Miss Dale; it is due very shortly, so please do not be long.'

Still bewildered and slightly fuddled with sleep, Francesca made no move, only stared at him. 'I really don't know what all this is about,' she told him, then shook her head in confusion. 'Is it very late? What time is breakfast?'

He obviously found her reply irritating, for he was frowning. 'Breakfast is at nine-thirty, Miss Dale. It is now six-thirty.' He glanced at the watch encircling his wrist, evidently wishing to be precise about it. 'In fact it is almost six-forty-five now, you were difficult to wake.'

'Six——' Francesca stared at him. Rubbing a hand over her dishevelled hair, she began to wonder if she might not still be dreaming. 'Are you telling me that it's only a quarter to seven? In the morning?'

'Of course!'

Francesca breathed slowly and deeply, trying to control her temper, for it had never been more sorely tried. 'I was asleep,' she told him in a voice that shook despite her attempts to steady it. 'I was travelling all day yesterday and part of the day before, and I'm tired! How dare you come hammering on my door at half-past six in the morning, you——'

'It was your wish that we—share and share alike, I believe that was the term you used,' he reminded her smoothly. 'And my day begins at six-thirty, Miss Dale.'

Francesca could see her own rashness coming home to roost in the most discomfiting manner possible, and she could have groaned aloud. Instead she looked at the man who stood there, issuing what was unmistakably a challenge and daring her to deny any of what he quoted. She believed she had never disliked anyone so much in her life.

'You took me literally, of course?' she asked, but saw her mild sarcasm fall on barren ground.

Her bottom lip was slightly unsteady, reproachful as the

eyes that still had the softness of sleep in them, and she began to understand, she thought. He had roused her from sleep to show her what could be in store for her, but he was not really serious about her getting up and going with him to see some wretched boat come in; he could not possibly be.

'I'm sorry,' she said, shaking her head at him, 'but you'll have to see the—green boat, or whatever, in on your own this morning. I'm really much too tired still, and I'm going back to sleep.'

That would have been the end of it as far as Francesca was concerned, and she closed the bedroom door. She closed it as far as it would go, then looked down in disbelief at the toe of a shiny brown riding boot that thrust into the gap and prevented it from going further. Raising wide and suddenly wary eyes, she found herself meeting a deep blue and very determined gaze that brought a sudden hard urgency to her heartbeat.

'Since you have stated very definitely that you wish to take an active part in running the estate, Miss Dale,' Antonio said in a cool, firm voice, 'I prefer that you begin without delay. You are already awake, and I doubt very much if you will be able to return to sleep, so if you will bathe and dress as quickly as possible I will delay my own departure until you are ready.' Once more that devastating gaze swept down over her lightly clad figure, missing nothing, she felt sure, especially the brightness of her colour. 'I assume half an hour will be time enough.'

Clutching the robe tightly because it suddenly felt very inadequate, she glared at him. 'You can assume what you like,' she retorted, 'but I'm not turning out at six-thirty in the morning, today or any other day! Now go away and leave me to sleep!'

He said something in Spanish, very short and very virulent, she guessed, and the look in his eyes was enough to send discomfiting shivers all along her spine. He seemed to tower over her and there was a taut, aggressive air of virility about him that touched other senses than fear too, so that she shrank back a little and passed a nervous tongue over her lips.

'We will have these matters determined from the beginning, Miss Dale.' He spoke in a voice that was deep and resonant, yet chillingly hard as steel, and the hardness was reflected in those disturbing blue eyes that watched her unwaveringly. 'I will make my feelings clear and then there will be no misunderstanding. I took over the running of Tradaro's when it was all but brought to ruin by mismanagement; Francis Dale had no real feeling for the place or for the job of running it, and he willingly allowed me to take over. For fifteen years I have worked it, as my family have worked it for generations, while Francis Dale simply reaped the profits. I did it because Tradaro's is mine by right of birth, and I anticipated that eventually it would come back to me. I will willingly work another fifteen or twenty years to keep it as prosperous as it is now, but I will not—I repeat *not*—support yet another useless member of your family, Miss Dale! Either you will sell me your share of the estate or you will work as I do to keep it the success it is now—do I make myself clear?'

Her head was swimming, but among the chaos of emotions Francesca recognised not only anger and indignation but a quite unexpected sympathy for the man facing her. If things had really been as he claimed, in her grandfather's time, then she could understand his feelings to some extent. What she could not forgive was his harshness in dealing with her as if it was her fault that the past fifteen years had culminated in bitter disappointment for him.

In her confusion she forgot about holding the robe together and it fell open showing the even flimsier covering underneath. Her hands pressed to her forehead she tried to think clearly; it was not the kind of confrontation one should be expected to face so early in the morning and after being woken from a deep sleep.

'I don't know anything about how things were when my grandfather was alive,' she reminded him, 'I didn't even know him. And you can't expect me to take responsibility for what he did—I wasn't there.'

His eyes watched her relentlessly. 'You are here now, Miss Dale, and if you are not prepared to share and share alike, as you suggested, may I again ask you to sell your share of the estate to me?'

It was all too quick, too unexpected, and Francesca was goaded to an automatic response because of that. She had so often dreamed during the past few months of owning a Caribbean island, and she was not ready to yield her bequest to anyone, and especially not to a man who seemed to have no qualms about exerting pressure to gain his own ends.

Lowering her hands slowly, she lifted her chin, and there was a gleam in her eyes he could not mistake. 'No, Mr Morales,' she said firmly, 'I *won't* sell you my share of Trader's Cay; not now, not ever!' Colour burned in her cheeks and the churning urgency of her heart showed quite clearly where the robe fell open and the soft swell of her breast fluttered in time with its beat. 'If I have to get up at six-thirty every morning for the rest of my life, I won't yield an inch to your sort of blackmail!'

His eyes noted that throbbing pulse with undisguised interest and she drew the robe together, holding it with trembling fingers and wondering where she had found the nerve to speak to him as she had. It was not the answer he expected, that much was clear from his expression, and she felt strangely elated at having called his bluff, although it was not the end of the matter, she was not naïve enough to think that. Men like Antonio Morales did not give up easily, and he was fighting for what he considered his own.

He stood there for a few seconds more, then bobbed his head in a curiously jerky little bow. 'I shall delay my departure until you are ready, Miss Dale,' he said. 'If we are to be partners then we shall be equal partners, make no mistake about it! And please do not keep me waiting too long!'

He turned swiftly and was gone, leaving Francesca staring after his tall angry figure as it strode along the landing without a backward glance. It would not even occur to him that she would do other than as he said, she realised, and it was annoying that she saw herself with little option.

Since it was to be a working day and she had no idea what would be expected of her, Francesca put on a short-sleeved cotton blouse and light slacks with a cotton square covering her hair and tied under at the back of her neck. It looked sufficiently businesslike, she thought, but at the same time was feminine and pretty, although it made her a little uneasy to realise that it was the very fact of that very distant and unapproachable aspect of Antonio Morales that gave her the desire to try and make an impression on him.

The house seemed very quiet, but she found someone to make her coffee and a fresh grapefruit, and was thrilled at the thought of it having come from her own estate. When she stepped out from under the porch, the sun was already hotter than when she first wakened and she caught her breath. But the garden smelled rich and scented with its mass of trees and shrubs and she thought wistfully of walking around it and savouring its beauty, if only she had not to see Antonio Morales. The temptation was there to ignore the meeting, but having gone so far to co-operate she saw no sense in not going all the way.

Instinct led her to the rear of the house, for those out-buildings she had spotted yesterday had suggested stables,

and Antonio had been dressed for riding, she thought. Sure
enough he was standing talking to a man who she assumed
was one of the stable workers, and his whole bearing suggested his patience was wearing thin. He had suggested that
half an hour was enough time, but it was almost an hour,
she noted, since he came banging on her bedroom door,
and the wait would not have improved his temper.

Francesca eyed him regretfully as she approached, for she
would really much rather have started off on tolerant terms
at least, and his frown gave little hope of that. They broke
off when she got nearer, and the man with him eyed her
with undisguised interest, a boldly speculative look in
rather mean dark eyes. Then Antonio said something to him
in Spanish and he nodded, disappearing into the building
behind him, while Antonio explained what he had in mind
for her to do.

'Garcia looks after the horses and he has saddled a small
gelding for you which I think will be suitable. When you
are ready we will go, for I am already very late.'

'You could have gone without me,' Francesca told
him, resenting the reprimand. 'And I'm sorry, but I don't
ride.'

It was apparent that her admission was the last straw and
he looked at her with narrowed eyes for a moment before
glancing over his shoulder at the man Garcia, returning
with two horses ready saddled. 'Without a horse it is impossible to cover the distances,' he told her. 'The island is
not large, Miss Dale, but it is too large to cover on foot, and
we do not have the time in any case. You will find riding a
horse quite simple once you have mastered the basic
principles.'

Garcia rejoined them, then stood waiting, his gnarled
hands holding the animals' reins and his eyes darting from
one to the other, detecting some kind of argument. Turning
suddenly, Antonio took the reins from him and dismissed

him with a few curt words, waiting until he had once more
disappeared into the stable building before he went on.

'The chestnut is yours. Come, I will show you how to
mount!'

'No!' Francesca backed away, finding the proximity of
the two animals too fearsome. 'I've never been on a horse
in my life, and you can't seriously mean me to just—get up
on one and go!'

Hard blue eyes watched her with a gleam of determination
in their depths, and she knew that he was quite serious
about it. He let go one rein, then turned again to Francesca,
who stood fighting down a feeling of panic. 'Come here!' A
peremptory hand summoned her closer, but she shook her
head.

Her knees were trembling, but she was angry too, for she
began to suspect the reason behind his insistence. What
better way to become the sole owner of Trader's Cay than
by persuading her to ride a horse when she did not even
know how to sit on one correctly? 'It won't work,' she told
him huskily, and went on to explain when he looked at her
with raised brows, 'You won't succeed in making me break
my neck, because I won't even get on the wretched thing!'

'Are you afraid, Miss Dale, or simply like your grandfather and cannot trouble yourself to learn?'

He asked the question softly, but it was a challenge and
Francesca was meant to recognise it as such, it was clear
enough in the way those blue eyes looked at her. She *was*
afraid, and she sympathised with her grandfather's un-
willingness to learn to ride, but she was not going to give
Antonio Morales any excuse at all. Tipping back her head,
she looked at him directly.

'Neither,' she insisted.

'Then come!' Again that commanding hand signalled her
nearer and this time she obeyed it almost as if she could not
help herself. 'I will lead you to begin with,' Antonio prom-

ised, and showed her how to grasp the saddle before cupping her foot in his hands and helping her up.

For a moment he stood looking at her, one hand on the horse's neck and the other on the back of the saddle. He was close enough for her to feel the warmth of his body pressed against her left leg and to be aware of a tangy mingling of masculine scents, and the thick wiry blackness of his hair. He reached up and eased her fingers on the rein, his hand firm but insistent when she instinctively kept her grip tight, then he caught her eye and once more that challenging gleam showed in their depths.

'Come!' he said, yet again, and turned swiftly to swing himself into the saddle of his own mount.

For just a second when he was no longer holding her, Francesca felt a moment of panic and her heart rapped away urgently at her side, making her breathless. Then he reached over and took her horse's curb rein, taking over control and keeping his own mount just slightly ahead so that the animal being led did not suffer too much discomfort.

In that way they rode sedately along the main track that the carriage had brought her yesterday, but where the scene was much different this morning. Ever side track leading on to the main one was filled with men lopping off the long stems of bananas with murderous-looking machetes which they wielded with apparent carelessness, and the main track itself was busy with the traffic of wooden, mule-drawn carts into which the fruit was placed for transport to the boxing sheds.

Had she been on foot Francesca had no doubt she would have found it all very interesting, but she was too intent on staying where she was to pay much attention to anything else. She heard the shouts that greeted Antonio as they passed, and sensed rather than saw the wide curious grins that recognised her as the new arrival of yesterday.

She was hot and shiny-faced before they reached the pier

at the far end of the track, and they were about twenty yards from the concrete apron when Antonio called a halt, and dismounted. He draped his horse's rein over a post, then came and stood beside her, looking up, his eyes half hidden by thick black lashes that seemed suddenly incongruous in such a very masculine face.

'I cannot delay any longer,' he informed her, 'so I shall leave you here, Miss Dale. There is a cargo going out, as you see, and I am certain that Perez will appreciate your help with checking. See him in the office in shed number one, and he will show you how to check the lading bill.'

Francesca had sudden visions of being left there in sole charge of the horse she rode, and while the animal seemed docile enough it would quite likely prove less amenable knowing there was an inexperienced hand on the rein. 'You're not going off and leaving me here?' she asked hastily, and detected the merest suggestion of a smile at the corner of his mouth.

'I will help you to dismount first and take care of the horse until you need it to ride back,' he promised. 'Now please hurry, Miss Dale, I have a busy morning ahead of me.'

Unaware of what was expected of her, she made no attempt to dismount in the usual way, but reached down with her arms to him as he stood there looking tall and strong and perfectly capable of lifting her out of the saddle. His moment of hesitation was scarcely noticeable, then he reached up his hands and put them beneath her arms, his palms clasping her warmly as he lifted her down, and retaining his hold for several seconds after she stood on the dusty track facing him.

She was conscious of a broad chest, dark and shadowy under the white shirt, and of the fiercely masculine body that touched against her with a tantalising lightness. His hands moved so very slightly, but she was aware of their pressure and of the sudden responsive impulse of her body before she stepped back quickly, her breathing not quite steady.

'I—I don't know what you want me to do,' she murmured, and hated the shivering lightness of her voice because it betrayed just how affected she had been by that deliberately provocative gesture.

'Perez in shed number one.' He repeated his earlier instructions while he remounted. 'You have to begin somewhere and marking the lading bill is as good a place as any! I shall be along in about one hour from now.'

'Oh, but wait, please!'

He took up the second rein and led her horse away, clucking his tongue to encourage the animals as he cut through one of the side tracks, then turned off almost at once and disappeared from sight. Bewildered and in growing anger at the treatment he had meted out to her so far that morning, Francesca glared at the grinning men, who seemed to find her being deserted cause for amusement.

There was nothing for it, she supposed, but to go on down to the sheds as he said, and see if she could find the man he mentioned. If she was to be put to work it might as well be on something that sounded a little more like the office work she was accustomed to, but she felt more alien than ever as she made her way among those smiling and curious dark faces.

The pier had seemed quite wide yesterday, but today, with a procession of women going back and forth, carrying cardboard cartons of fruit on the outward journey, it seemed much smaller and in danger of collapse under the weight of traffic. The noises was unbelievable too, and none of it intelligible to her, so that she hesitated before asking the man she sought.

'Mr—Señor Payreth?' She ventured the question several times, but with no success until a young boy came over and stood grinning up at her, his bright, dark eyes more friendly than any she had seen so far. 'Can *you* tell me where I can find Señor Payreth?' she asked, and the boy's grin widened until it almost divided his face into two.

'Señor Perez?' he said, and when she heard his pronunciation of the unfamiliar Spanish, Francesca realised why she had gone so long uninformed. The boy pointed a finger in the direction of a small glass-fronted box. 'He is there, *señorita.*'

She could see no one actually in the office, but now that she knew where to look she felt less at a loss and she smiled her thanks at the boy. She had turned and was about to push through the mass of bodies to the little glass box when she heard her name called and turned back quickly. Thankful that Antonio Morales had been less than the hour he estimated, she admitted to being glad to see him.

But it was not Antonio's face she caught sight of for a moment before it vanished again behind the endless procession of cardboard cartons, it was Andrés, and when she realised he was making his way through to her, Francesca felt a curious uneasiness. He was smiling and she suspected that Andrés Morales was far more likely to smile like that at the thought of her discomfiture than because he was pleased to see her.

He stood beside her, one hand holding a clip-board and the other a pen, and his dark eyes quizzed her curiously. 'You are abroad early this morning, Miss Dale,' he said, in the same neat and pedantic form of English that his father used.

He looked somehow younger this morning, and perhaps slightly less malicious than he had on their first encounter, but he was not someone she could claim to like, and when he pulled her forward quickly out of the way of a passing truck, she caught her breath. He noticed it and Francesca was sure he smiled, but she was having to concentrate on what he was saying above the din in the shed and couldn't be sure.

'Why are you here, Miss Dale? Is my father with you?'

'I'm here on his orders,' Francesca told him, making no attempt to hide the fact that she was not there from choice. 'I am to see Señor—Pay——'

'Perez,' said Andrés, taking her up hastily. 'Your accent is not very good, Miss Dale.'

'I don't speak Spanish,' Francesca informed him with a touch of asperity. 'I didn't know I'd need to!'

She noticed then that while he was speaking to her, he was also keeping an eye on the procession of people carrying out the loaded cartons of fruit, and as he watched he made small ticks on the board he carried. How he kept track, Francesca had no idea, for it seemed utter chaos to her, and she came to the conclusion that perhaps Andrés Morales was more quick-witted and intelligent than her first impression suggested.

'You have to see Perez about—what?' he asked, and Francesca felt a small stirring of resentment because he sounded all too much like that older Morales, and very nearly as autocratic.

'I'm to take an active part in running the estate,' she told him, and realised as she said it that she got a certain amount of satisfaction out of telling him. 'I'm to start here, checking something that's known as a lading bill, I believe.'

Andrés showed her the board he held and smiled broadly. 'I am so glad,' he told her. 'It is something I dislike intensely but I also have been made to begin at the bottom of the ladder, Miss Dale, although it would seem rather a waste of time in the circumstances. Will you take it from me?'

He held out the board, but Francesca backed away, shaking her head, appalled at the idea of being plunged so deeply into what was evidently quite an important part of the procedure, at this stage. 'Oh, no!' she protèsted. 'I'd prefer to watch you for a while, until I at least know what's going on.'

Andrés showed his teeth in another smile, and it seemed incredible, seeing the gleam in his eyes, that he was barely eighteen years old; he had an air of malice that ill suited his handsome features and made him appear much older. 'Are you not afraid of what my father will say when he comes and finds that you are not doing as he told you?' he asked, and the implication he managed to put into the question brought a flush to Francesca's face.

'I'm not easily frightened, Andrés,' she told him, and did not care if her dislike was quite obvious. 'You should know that.'

She deliberately referred to his dangerous stupidity of yesterday, and realised as she did so that she had never discovered whether or not Antonio had administered the tit-for-tat punishment he had threatened his son with. Cecilia Morales had seemed to think he was quite capable of dealing with Andrés as Andrés had dealt with his horse, but Francesca could not bring herself to believe that of him.

Andrés accepted the reference to his behaviour without embarrassment or apology, and it occurred to Francesca to wonder whether he had after all got off scot free. 'I'd made up my mind to tell you exactly what I thought of your idiotic stunt yesterday,' she told him, 'but your father assured me he would deal with you in his own way. Did he—deal with you?'

'If you are asking whether he thrashed me as he threatened to,' Andrés told her, 'I think I can guess what you are hoping is true! I imagine Abuela told you about that,' he added with a knowing smile. 'She was concerned about it.'

'Quite naturally,' Francesca told him, and expressed her own opinion more harshly because his manner and uncaring brashness annoyed her. 'But in my opinion, whatever your father did to you, you deserved!'

'Then I am sorry to disappoint you, señorita!' His eyes resented her deliberate harshness, even though he was smiling again. 'Oh, my father is perfectly capable of doing as he said he would, and he would not hesitate to do so but for one thing. I have a—a certain advantage which I do not hesitate to make use of when necessary, and this was one of those occasions.' He waited, almost as if he expected a reaction, but when Francesca said nothing, he went on, 'You see, Miss Dale, I am my father's only child, his only son, and it is important to him that I remain here to take over Tradaro's from him—in due time, of course!'

It was somewhat disturbing to realise that yet again she felt a kind of sympathy with Antonio Morales, although she found it hard to account for, even to herself. She knew nothing about his wife, beyond the fact that she had been dead for a number of years, but knowing how he felt about Trader's Cay she could well believe that he set great store by his only son. A fact that Andrés was obviously fully aware of.

He was laughing softly, as if at some great private joke and his eyes showed gleamingly dark as he watched her face. 'My father looks to me to continue the Morales tradition here on Tradaro's,' he told her, 'and if I should decide to return to Madrid and remain there, near my maternal grandparents, then he will have lost his only heir and his hope of continuing the tradition. He can imagine nothing worse than that!'

'And you'd go!' said Francesca, without for a minute doubting it.

Andrés curled his lip derisively, scorning her opinion. 'My father believes I would, Miss Dale, that is the important thing!' He stood and mused on the idea as if it afforded him great satisfaction. 'He could marry again, but I do not think marriage appeals to him very much. That is not to say he does not like women,' he added with another bark of laughter. 'He may even be tempted to marry you, for then he could gain complete control of Tradaro's. Have you thought of that, Miss Dale?'

He thrust the clip-board and pen into her hands and, without waiting for a reaction, turned and walked swiftly away to be lost in the bustle and clamour of the shed. Francesca's head was swimming, although she told herself that such an outrageous situation as Andrés Morales suggested was completely out of the question. What she did not understand at all was the part of her that toyed with the idea of it being true and considered it with a curious kind of excitement rather than revulsion.

It was several minutes before she began to realise that she had been left in charge of the list she held and had so far done nothing about it. If she could have remedied the situation, she would have, even though Andrés had not marked it since their conversation began, but she had no idea what she was required to do and the procession of cartons continued to travel endlessly through the shed and out on to the pier to the waiting boats.

She must find the elusive Perez and seek his help, and with that in mind she looked around for the tiny glass box of an office she had seen earlier. Having located it she was in the act of turning to make her way there when a hand fell on her arm and she gasped aloud, turning wide and startled eyes on Antonio Morales.

'Miss Dale!' He took the board she held and stood frowning over it, while Francesca simply watched and made no attempt as yet to explain what had happened. Flicking through the pages, he pursed his lips, his opinion in little doubt. 'I find it difficult to believe that our figures are so much down this morning, Miss Dale. Are you certain none have been missed? You were about to leave when I arrived, I believe—was something wrong?'

If only she could have banished that disturbing suggestion of Andrés' she would have felt better able to cope with his questions, Francesca felt. But as it was she found his sudden presence quite alarmingly affecting and shook her head a little dazedly in response. 'I was going to find Señor—the man you told me to ask.'

He was frowning over the list again, obviously not interested in explanations. 'Perhaps you find the task too much for you?' he suggested. 'I find it hard to believe you are not capable of marking off a list, Miss Dale; or perhaps Perez did not give you sufficient instruction? I can think of no other reason for you failing to do it correctly.'

It was the last straw as far as Francesca was concerned, she had reached the limit of her patience. Both father and son had tried her beyond endurance, she felt, and she would take no more from either of them. Her face was flushed with the unbearable heat of the shed, and her head ached with the clamour of unintelligible Spanish going on all around her. Tilting her chin at an angle so that she looked up in to his face, she glared at Antonio angrily.

'I can't be expected to cope with work I've never done before,' she told him. She was trembling with anger, she realised, and fearful lest she burst into tears of sheer frustration and confirm his opinion of her as hopeless. 'If you weren't trying so hard to make me give up and go home, you wouldn't have thrown me in at the deep end like this! Well, I've no intention of taking any more of your bullying, Mr Morales—yours or you son's! Excuse *me*!'

At that point Francesca would have made what she considered was a very dignified exit in the circumstances, but once more his hand was laid on her arm and his long fingers pressed into her flesh. 'I allotted you a task that any school-child could have done efficiently,' Antonio told her harshly, 'and the fact that you have made such a dismal failure of it suggests to me that you are likely to be of no more use than your grandfather was, Miss Dale. I——'

He was cut short when Francesca's open palm connected with his cheek; a hard resounding slap that made his head jerk right round, and tipped a thick swathe of black hair over one eye. A dozen people nearby saw what happened, but Francesca did not stop to find out what the outcome was, she made her way swiftly and half blindly through the busy shed into the open.

The sun dazzled her and she squinted behind a raised hand while she got her bearings, then set off across the concrete towards the main track. She might have been simply crying with temper, Francesca wished she knew, but she brushed the tears from her eyes impatiently and set off at a fairly fast walk along the dusty track. Heaven knew why she felt so much like crying, or why her legs seemed so unsteady, for she would not admit to being afraid of Antonio Morales, no matter how angry he was going to be at being slapped in public.

She noticed nothing of what was going on around her as she made her way back towards the house, only moving automatically to one side whenever one of the wooden carts came up behind her. She could not see at the moment just where the situation with Antonio was going to end, and it troubled her more than she cared to admit. She could have explained how she had not seen Perez, but been thrust into the position without instruction of any kind, by his son. Instead she had slapped him hard and in front of his own people, and he was not the kind of man to overlook such treatment, nor easily forgive it.

Because she could not be sure whether or not she would find Andrés with his grandmother, she turned off from the track at the last minute and made her way across the grass land to where she supposed the sea to be. She saw no reason why she should not find that quiet beach she had promised herself, and sit there for a while until she recovered her composure and could think clearly.

Beyond a strip of shrubs and flowering trees she discovered the palm-fringed beach she sought, and for a moment or two the pleasure of it overcame her unhappiness and she

smiled. The border of palms went almost to the ocean's
edge, and between them it was cool and shady, with a light
wind stirring the fringed leaves overhead and rippling
through the white sand at her feet.

It was every bit as good as she had anticipated it would be,
and for several minutes she put everything else out of her
mind and enjoyed it. Not for very long, though, for gradu-
ally the thought of Andrés' deliberate malice came back to
disturb her enjoyment, and of Antonio's scornful reference
to her being like her grandfather. She had a right to be
angry, she thought, and pulled the scarf from her head
suddenly, shaking out her fiery red hair in an unwitting
gesture of defiance.

She leaned against one of the hairy brown trunks with her
hands tucked behind her back and gazed at the glittering
ocean with half-closed eyes. She could challenge Antonio to
call her useless by setting out to learn all she could, and in
some way make up for her grandfather's shortcomings, or
she could ask for the very highest price for her share and go
back to England. But somehow the second idea was unac-
ceptable, and she shook her head firmly, convinced she
would never do that.

She seemed not to have been there more than a few
minutes when she became aware of a horse somewhere close
by, and inevitably that meant either Andrés or his father. At
the moment she was unsure which one she wanted to see
least, and in any case she resisted the impulse to turn around
and find out.

How she realised it was Antonio without seeing him, she
did not know, but a few seconds later he walked round in
front of her and confirmed her guess. Her heart was hammering hard, for she did not believe he would easily con-
done her slapping him, however justified she felt she was.
When she glanced up at him after a moment or two she saw
that the mark of her hand stood out vividly on his tanned

cheek and realised how hard she must have hit him. Without any reason at all, she was suddenly sorry she had done it, and at the same time annoyed with herself for being sorry.

She noticed how hard he gripped the Spanish leather quirt in his long hands and flicked him another uneasy glance. His temper was every bit as fiery as her own, she believed, and he was not the type of man to relish being slapped in public by a woman. Andrés, by speaking as he had of that nonsensical idea of marrying her to gain the other half of Trader's Cay, had made her selfconscious too, and she shifted uneasily under his scrutiny.

'If I did not realise that you had good reason to be angry, I would make you regret that slap,' he said after an interminable time, and Francesca automatically looked up quickly her chin set at an angle, but he allowed her no time to reply. 'But if you ever do such a thing again you may be sure you *will* regret it, *señorita*! Do I make myself clear?'

Her cheeks flaming and her eyes brightly defiant, Francesca still managed to hold his gaze, though it was becoming increasingly hard to do so. 'I don't like being jeered at and made to feel useless when I've done nothing to deserve it,' she told him, and lowered her eyes at last. 'I—I suppose I shouldn't have slapped you like that, not there where everyone could see, but you *did* ask for it.'

'You could have told me that you had not seen Perez and had received no instruction,' Antonio declared firmly. 'It would have served more purpose and been less—childish.'

'Childish!' Francesca stared at him, her cheeks burning. 'You dare to——'

'I dare to suggest that you act without thinking, Miss Dale, and I do not intend being the victim of your bad temper!'

'You didn't give me a chance to say *anything*!' Francesca insisted. 'You were so intent on telling me how lazy my

grandfather was, and how like him I am, that you didn't
want to hear *why* I wasn't checking the silly list!'

'I know why—now,' Antonio told her. 'Perez told me
that he saw nothing of you, but that Andrés was checking
the lading list. You presumably took it over from him.'

'I didn't, as a matter of fact.' She was reluctant, even now,
to make more bad blood between him and Andrés, and yet
if she was to justify her own position there was little else
she could do. She eased herself away from the palm tree
and walked almost to the edge of the water, keeping her
back to him while she spoke. 'Andrés—dislikes me,' she said.
'And he's even less subtle about showing it than you are.'

'He is a boy.'

He sounded as if he made it an excuse, but being so few
years older than Andrés, she did not accept his age as
vindication. 'He must be about eighteen,' she insisted. 'He's
not a child, and to my mind the things he does are far less
excusable than my slapping your face, although you considered that childish.'

She sought the support of another palm, tucking her
hands behind her once again, and wriggling her fingers in
the rough hairiness of the trunk. It was a posture that
emphasised the soft roundness of her figure and made nonsense of the childish theory, although she was not aware of
it at the moment, or even of the dark blue eyes that took
such explicit note of it and glowed more darkly.

'He did not tell you how to mark the lading bill?' he
asked, and Francesca shook her head. 'And you think I
should punish him for trying to—make things more difficult
for you?'

Francesca shrugged uneasily, aware now of the eyes
watching her from below those thick concealing lashes. She
eased herself away from the tree and brushed down her
slacks with hands that trembled slightly. He was the most
disturbing man she had ever had contact with, and that sly,

outrageous intimation of Andrés' again slipped into her mind and troubled her.

'I don't want anyone punished,' she said in a small and rather unsteady voice. 'I just want to—to be allowed to enjoy what my grandfather gave to me in his will. The only thing he ever gave me, as a matter of fact.'

'And you will not even consider selling your share to me?'

He seemed suddenly more close and she was touched by the effect of that overpowering virility that seemed an integral part of him, whatever his mood. Looking up at him, she tossed back her hair, brushing it back with her hands as she angled her chin. 'No!' she declared firmly. 'I won't sell it, and nothing you say or do will make me change my mind!'

For what seemed like an interminable time he held her gaze and there was something in his deep blue eyes that made the blood run faster through her veins and her heart skip with an uncontrollable flutter of excitement. 'We shall see,' he said softly, and Francesca looked away, starting back slightly when he extended a hand towards her. 'It is time for breakfast,' he said, and she noticed he was smiling.

CHAPTER THREE

IT was hard to believe that she had been there for more than a week, and Francesca had to admit that she seemed to have fitted into the Morales household with rather less trouble than she had anticipated. Andrés still unmistakably resented her presence, but he made his feelings less actively obvious, so that she suspected his father had had something to say on the subject. But he was still uncommunicative and never addressed her directly if he could help it.

Cecilia Morales proved to be a gentle and kind but rather

ineffectual woman, and Francesca could see how she would have found it impossible to run the estate on her own after her husband died. Unlike her son she was not island born, but had come as a bride to Trader's Cay nearly forty years before. It was the custom, she told Francesca, for the Morales to choose their wives from the old country, and she had been as excited as Francesca herself at the prospect of coming to a Caribbean island. Whether or not she had ever had cause to change her opinion was something she did not mention, and it wasn't something that Francesca could ask.

Francesca had never needed to be roused again at six-thirty, although she did occasionally linger for a while longer, ten or fifteen minutes, just for the satisfaction of defying Antonio's timetable. She had proved quite an adept pupil on horseback too, although she still had a lot to learn, and Antonio was not the most patient of men. Consequently she sought the help of Garcia, the stable man, sometimes and found him less unco-operative than first acquaintance had suggested.

Ever since that first morning, it had become normal practice for her to meet Antonio in the stable yard where he would see her safely mounted and ride with her as far as the beginning of the plantation, leaving her with some fairly simple task to do before riding off on his own more urgent business. It was never anything very difficult that he left her to do, but it justified her claiming to help with the running of the place, and only in the last couple of days had it dawned on Francesca that he was breaking her in very gently—much more so than her first opinion of him had suggested he would.

She had been there for just over a week when he told her one morning that he had to leave right away and attend to some minor disaster in the boxing sheds. It would be an idea, he told her, if she rode as far as Punta Salida, the farthest tip of the island, and get some idea of just how extensive the estate was. He would join her there later on and ride back with her in time for breakfast.

It seemed ridiculous to think she missed his company for those few minutes' ride out of the stable yard and across the open grassland, but strangely enough she did. He was arrogant and had little patience with her lack of skill on horseback, but somehow he was a reassuring companion with whom to start the day.

Hearing another horse coming up behind her, she half turned, rather awkwardly, and recognised Andrés racing towards her on the black mare he most often favoured. Seeing him coming so fast Francesca felt a flick of panic when she recalled his deliberate and ruthless panicking of the carriage horse. She could never bring herself to entirely trust Andrés.

He rode with such style that she could not help but feel a twinge of envy, wondering if she would ever be as proficient as he undeniably was, despite his recklessness and the harshness with which he used his animals. He pulled the black mare to a halt right alongside her own mount and beamed her a smile; a smile that did nothing to reassure her, but rather made her suspect he had something unpleasant in mind.

He was incredibly handsome, and Cecilia had told her that Andrés had inherited her Welsh grandfather's looks, although not his blue eyes as Antonio had. It was a pity, Francesca thought, that he put himself out to be so determinedly unfriendly and resentful, because his youth and dark good looks did not prepare the unwary for his less attractive characteristics. Nevertheless she smiled a little warily in response to his greeting and held the gelding steady when he rode up close beside her.

'What orders have you been given for this morning?' he asked, and Francesca felt the colour warm her cheeks as she kept facing determinedly forward.

'Your father suggested I ride out towards Punta Salida,' she told him.

'And naturally you will do as you are told!'

His voice was quiet, almost seductive in its softness, and yet Francesca felt a trickle of warning along her spine. If only she had the nerve and the ability to put heels to her horse's flanks and simply ride away from him! Instead she kept her eyes forward and angled her chin, her interest apparently on the towering forest of banana plants ahead.

'I've no reason not to in this instance,' she told him, then turned and noticed his faint smile. 'You don't have to wait for me, Andrés, I can manage alone, thank you.'

He murmured something in Spanish, then leaned across and placed one hand on the horse's back behind her, his smile broadening as he looked into her face. 'You are very pretty, Miss Dale, but not very—encouraging.'

His sudden apparent desire to be friendly aroused even more wariness, and Francesca's heart fluttered uneasily when the gelding she rode made a sudden and unexpected gyration with its hindquarters. Probably the unexpected hand on its back made it uneasy, and she tried not to pull on the rein, which was the instinctive thing to do. She hated the idea of Andrés seeing her alarmed, and made her voice as matter-of-fact as possible.

'I'm not being discouraging, Andrés,' she told him, 'but please don't lean like that, you're scaring my horse.'

'This cow!' He slapped the gelding's rump disdainfully, and the animal again skittered nervously. 'It is fit only for the slaughterhouse!' He caught her anxious eye and laughed, his own eyes gleaming darkly as he sat back straight in his saddle. 'Very well, ride alone if that is what you prefer, *señorita*! *Adiós!*'

He jabbed in his heels and the black mare took off like the wind, with the sting of his quirt to drive her faster, his laughter carrying back to her and making Francesca shudder. She watched him take the main dirt road down to the pier, and thanked heaven he was not going in the same direction as she was.

The departure of Andrés, however, did nothing to soothe the gelding and he was if anything more fractious than ever, jerking and shaking and alarmingly unco-operative. His back, instead of accommodating her comfortably as it normally did, was arched, and it was all she could do to stay up. She sought to hold him, but quite suddenly all control was out of her hands, and the horse took off, careering wildly as he ran, bucking and jerking and completely uncontrollable.

Terrified, Francesca clung to him as best she could, unable to do anything but pray she wouldn't be thrown off, while the gelding headed for a narrow and mostly unused track right at the far side of the rows of tall ragged banana plants. A strip of jungle-like growth divided the plantation from the palm-fringed beach and gave brief glimpses of the sparkling blue ocean, but Francesca saw none of it as she hung on for her very life.

It was nothing like an ordinary straightforward gallop, for the gelding was behaving with frenzied savagery, trying to unseat her, and as they raced erratically along the track, brushing the overhanging trees, the creature stiffened his legs again and tossed her away. One foot caught briefly in the stirrup and she was dragged several feet before her shoe was wrenched off and she fell on to the track and lay still.

The next thing Francesca noticed was the dappling shadows that allowed blinding spots of light across her eyes before being blotted out again. Someone knelt beside her and a familiar face swam into view, an expression between anger and concern flitting across the dark strong features, while a hand brushed the hair back from her forehead with unbelievably gentle fingers.

'Miss Dale?' The same light touch brushed down her

cheek and she opened her mouth to say something, forgot what it was, and licked her dry lips instead. 'Miss Dale! Francesca!'

She didn't hurt, which puzzled her, but she felt weak and limp and incredibly heavy-headed, and she rolled her head sideways to look up at the first sign of compassion she had yet seen on Antonio Morales' face. 'I——' Her voice scratched dryly in her throat and she licked her lips again, longing for something cool. 'The horse——'

'I found the horse,' Antonio told her, precise as usual, 'that is how I knew something had happened to you. And also you were seen coming this way riding very fast, so I was told.' The deep voice shivered with unexpected passion as he glowered down at her. '*Madre de Dios!* What were you trying to do, riding so fast?'

'He—ran away with me.' She saw the frown that flicked between his black brows. 'I don't know—I don't know what frightened him, but I couldn't——'

'That is enough talking!' He silenced her with a long finger laid across her lips and the burning touch of his flesh on her face brought unexpected and more violent reaction from her senses. 'We must discover how badly you are hurt. Can you move your legs?'

Francesca lay just as she had fallen and he made no attempt to move her, but watched her face with a curious intentness as he knelt beside her. She had one arm across her breast and the other was down at her side, while her legs were stretched out in front, one foot minus its shoe. Flexing each leg in turn, she discovered that apart from some minor discomfort which could be caused by bruising, they appeared to be undamaged. Her left arm too gave only a minor twinge when she moved it, but when she attempted to do the same with her right arm she gasped at a searing pain that ran through its whole length.

She bit hard on her lower lip to stop herself from crying,

although shock and pain made it difficult, and she kept her eyes lowered so that Antonio should not see how misty they looked. 'Your right arm?' he asked, and she nodded, then caught her breath audibly when he touched it only very lightly. 'All right,' he soothed, and when he turned his head to address someone behind him, she realised that he had not come alone.

About a dozen of the field workers had gathered and stood watching, dark eyes both curious and sympathetic. At a word from Antonio one of the men broke a stave from one of the wooden crates and handed it to him, presumably for use as a makeshift splint. Watching her closely, he held the stave in his hand and spoke softly, for her ears alone.

'It will hurt,' he warned, and placed the splintery surface of the wood against her inner arm. 'I will try to make it as little as possible, yes?' Again Francesca nodded silently, and he glanced up at the group crowding in on them more closely. '*Un bufanda,*' he said. '*No, dos bufandas, pronto!*'

Immediately two of the women hastened to untie the scarves they wore around their heads, and handed them over, then stood grinning selfconsciously and rubbing their hands over close-cropped heads. With the primitive tools at his command, Antonio made a very passable job of binding her injured arm, and Francesca bore the not inconsiderable pain it caused her without making a murmur.

When he was finished the limb was immobile, straight down at her side, and he looked at her enquiringly. 'O.K.?' Apart from a nagging ache that seemed to encompass her whole body, she seemed to have come off very lightly in the circumstances, Francesca supposed, and again she nodded agreement. 'Then in a moment or two we will try to get you on to your feet, eh?'

'Yes, of course. I can manage now if you help me.'

He slipped an arm around her, keeping her injured one firmly to her side as he practically lifted her off the ground and he murmured something in Spanish when she gasped with pain. It seemed as if every bone in her body had been battered with a club, and the broken arm hurt so much that it almost demolished her determined self-control.

Somehow she got to her feet, then she stood for a moment with Antonio's supporting arm still around her, and the urge to lean against the broad chest so conveniently near was irresistible. Her head drooped and she laid her cheek on a soft white shirt, her eyes closed and strangely content to remain there, for all her pain.

His body generated a heat that burned her like fire and filled her with a curious feeling of anticipation. His arm still encircled her, firm and protective as she half turned towards him with her face buried against his chest, and one big hand rested on the curve of her breast, finger-tips exerting the very lightest pressure. That brief, light touch was the only recognition he made of her as a woman, and when he spoke she dragged herself reluctantly back to practicalities.

'It is too far for you to walk back to the house,' he said, speaking so that only she heard what he said, 'therefore I have sent for the *carruaje* to be brought for you. Unfortunately it is not possible to bring it this far and you will have to walk along the feeder road—can you manage that?'

'Yes, I think so.'

In fact the very idea of walking anywhere did not appeal at all, but it was thoughtful of him to have sent for the carriage. 'You will appreciate that it is very difficult to get a doctor here,' Antonio went on, 'but I have asked that my mother ring Doctor Juarez in San Juan and I am certain he will oblige. He has the use of a helicopter and it takes not very long to fly.'

'That's very good of you.'

Francesca was feeling slightly lightheaded, and it seemed almost irresistible to suggest that no one would surely have the nerve to refuse a summons from Antonio Morales. For the first time she became aware that the situation of being held in that firmly encircling arm was rather intimate when surrounded by a circle of dark and frankly interested faces, and she tried to ease away slightly, catching her lower lip between her teeth when the movement, however slight, made her feel she had been kicked.

'Your—the people——' She glanced up when his arm was removed with apparent reluctance and caught a faintly quizzical look that made her more selfconscious than ever.

'I apologise, Miss Dale.' He spoke so softly that no one else could possibly have heard, but still it gave Francesca the feeling that he found her reaction rather amusing, possibly even naïve. 'Will you not sit down? I am sure you are not very steady on your own feet.'

'*Señorita, con su permiso!*' Francesca turned and saw a smiling face below a straw hat, a gesturing hand indicating something immediately behind her and a wooden crate was pressed persuasively against the back of her knees. 'Please to sit, yes?'

She sat gratefully, and smiled her thanks at the donor, turning back to find that one of the women had recovered her shoe lost in the fall, and was kneeling to replace it for her. Again she smiled her thanks, and it occurred to her that this was the first time she had actually been made to feel as if she belonged. It was a sensation that did a great deal to make her feel better, and she looked up at Antonio Morales to see what his opinion was.

As it so often was, his expression was indecipherable, but he nodded his head briefly and said something to the provider of the crate. It must have been an injunction to return to work, for the little group who had been clustered around them began to drift away, chattering among themselves cheerfully. Francesca found it food for thought, the fact that they obeyed so unhesitatingly and without rancour, for it once more made her feel that she had been transported into quite another world. Antonio's power over his people seemed to her more modern eye to be almost feudal, and yet no one questioned it. He was an autocrat in the old tradition, a ruthless man at times, and yet Francesca believed he could be gentle too, and the mingling of the two was curiously attractive.

Leaving her sitting on the wooden crate, he walked across to where the two horses were tethered and was running his hands over the gelding, frowning slightly. The glossy hide had sweated profusely and it flinched in response to the familiar hand, but the moment he pressed a hand on to the saddle as he bent to look at the girth strap the animal gyrated its hindquarters just as it had with Francesca in the saddle.

Soothing words in Spanish subdued the creature in part, but it rolled a wary eye when Antonio began to undo the cinch, swivelling round and tugging its head against the rein that held it tethered to a tree. The saddle was lifted and placed on the ground, then a long hand reached and took something from the animal's back. Antonio held it in his palm and when he turned and faced Francesca again he was frowning fiercely, a dark gleaming look in his eyes.

Francesca felt the drumming of her pulse as he crossed the short space between them, and she looked up at him anxiously when he stopped beside her. 'What—what is it?' she ventured, and watched his face still, rather than look at what he had in his hand.

She had seen him angry more times than she cared to remember in the brief time she had known him, but she thought she had never seen him look quite as he did now. Something about him made her tremble and it was hard to try and think as clearly as she wanted to. He stood below the mop-like shadow of a palm tree and its flitting, striated light and shade gave added severity to his expression as he opened his hand and showed her what lay in the palm of it.

It was a small spiny burr of some kind, and where he had held it, little touches of blood from the gelding's back speckled his fingers. It looked so viciously cruel that Francesca caught her breath, imagining the torture that the gelding must have endured before he managed to unseat her. And she could come to no other conclusion than the one she did, although she was not yet ready to place the blame where she believed it belonged.

'I—I had no idea——' she began, but Antonio's scornful gesture cut her short.

'Of course you did not!' he retorted harshly. 'I am not such a fool as to imagine you would risk breaking your own neck, Miss Dale! And I credit you with more intelligence than to believe you see me as the culprit; even though you have suggested I might have it in mind!'

Francesca said nothing, and he concentrated his attention on her until she avoided looking up at all costs. He was the most disconcerting inquisitor she had ever had to face, and he suspected that she knew, or at least had some good idea, of who was responsible, that was clear. She jerked her head up nervously when he set one booted foot on the crate immediately behind her and leaned forward, bringing his face close, and enveloping her in the virile warmth of his body.

'But I think you know who *is* responsible,' he insisted.

'So do you!'

She felt sure he did, and when she glanced briefly upward for just a moment, a certain look she saw in his eyes confirmed it. Nevertheless she felt no special desire to tell him what he waited to hear, but instead sought to stave off the inevitable. For one thing she felt an odd reluctance to tell him something that she was convinced he already knew but still hoped to have denied.

'I—I don't believe Garcia would——' she began.

'Garcia would *not*!' he agreed with swift certainty. 'And

please do not prevaricate, *señorita*; I wish to know the truth, and I believe you can confirm my own suspicion!'

At once repelled and fascinated by his relentless insistence, Francesca obeyed. 'I—I met Andrés just after I left the stable; actually he caught me up and rode along with me for—I don't know exactly, a minute or two at most.'

'And?'

'While we rode together he—he leaned across and put one hand on the gelding's back, behind me. I couldn't see if he did anything or not, but the gelding—shied away from him, and just after that Andrés rode off alone.'

'You saw no one else?'

He still clung to the hope that it need not prove to be his son after all, Francesca realised, and did not altogether understand her own reluctance to prove it otherwise. Why she should care one way or the other about either of them was beyond her, but whereas she would have had little compunction about blaming Andrés, she wished that by doing so she did not have to hurt the proud yet strangely vulnerable man beside her. It was an emotion she did not begin to understand, but she found it oddly disturbing.

'I saw no one else,' she confirmed. 'And from the moment he put his hand on him the gelding started—playing up, and eventually threw me.'

Antonio stood looking at the burr in his hand, then he flung it from him with a gesture of disgust, his booted foot thudding on to the dry earth. He carried the same kind of red Spanish quirt that Andrés always used, and he lashed in vicious fury suddenly at the palm tree beside him, the blow stripping the bark from its trunk and leaving a strip of bare wood.

'He goes too far!' he rasped harshly, and Francesca shuddered.

There was a savagery about him that she found alarming and she brushed a moistening tongue across dry lips. She remembered how confident Andrés had been that he could successfully counter any threat of violence his father made, and suspected that in this instance he had over-estimated his power to blackmail.

'Please,' she ventured, without stopping to consider why he should take the slightest notice of anything she said. 'Please don't—don't do anything while you're so angry.' Her eyes were on the riding whip and he noticed it, lifting it so that it was held as if ready for use.

'So,' he said quietly, 'you have been told of my threat to thrash him?'

Francesca shook her head, unwilling to get too deeply involved and yet anxious that he should not do anything he would almost surely regret later. Strangely she felt that she was more anxious for him than for Andrés, and that did not make much sense either. His eyes were narrowed until they were merely a glimmer of brilliant blue between dark lashes, and his mouth was hard and firm, a straight ruthless line in the dark Spanish face.

'Why is it that you are suddenly pleading for Andrés?' he asked, but she noticed how much less harsh his voice was than the expression on his face.

It was hard to explain, and she was beginning to feel alarmingly unsteady as she sat there on the wooden crate. Her body ached and her right arm hurt naggingly so that she held it close to her side with her left hand. It was possibly delayed shock combined with the heat and the discomfort of her injuries that made her feel slightly faint suddenly, but she must have paled considerably, for Antonio noticed and bent over her, anxiety momentarily replacing anger.

'Francesca?' His hand rested on her shoulder and he looked into her face, the warmth of his body pressed close for a moment. 'Are you feeling faint?' He glanced up before she could reply, for a man came hurrying along the feeder road opposite where she sat. 'Ah!' Antonio said with obvious satisfaction. 'The *carruaje* is here. Can you make it to the end of the feeder road?'

Francesca nodded, her teeth clamped hard over her bottom lip as she fought hard against the encroaching tears. It was self-pity, it had to be, but she had never felt more weak and shocked in her life as Antonio once again slipped his arm around her and helped her to her feet. She did not look up, but stood for a moment in the curve of his supporting arm, anticipating that walk along between the plants to the main track.

'I am sorry if you are embarrassed, Francesca,' he said in a firm and determined voice, 'but I am going to carry you— it will be much quicker!' Beyond a faint gasp when he slid his other arm beneath her legs and lifted her with apparent ease, Francesca said nothing, but she relaxed with a sense of relief against the reassuring breadth of his chest when he held her in his arms, and automatically placed her left arm around his neck. 'It will be better,' Antonio said, 'if you use your free hand to support your broken one.'

She caught his eye briefly and felt a familiar twinge of resentment, but she did as he said, and with the messenger leading the two horses and bringing up the rear, they started along the rough track. Always selfconscious about being the centre of attraction, Francesca felt herself colour furiously under the benign but unmistakably amused eyes that followed their progress every inch of the way. It couldn't be very often, she guessed, that Antonio Morales went striding through his estate with a woman in his arms.

By looking up through her lashes it was possible to study his face at close quarters while he carried her, and she found the study fascinating. Tiny lines at the corners of his eyes were a revelation, and so was an unexpectedly deep dimple in one lean cheek that she had never noticed before, probably because he so seldom smiled. His mouth was wide and less thin-lipped than she had thought, and relaxed it was quite good-humoured.

It was a fascinating face and she found pleasure in taking surreptitious stock of it until she realised he in turn was watching her. 'I am unaccustomed to being studied quite so minutely, Miss Dale,' he said, but while his voice suggested disapproval Francesca noticed a faint gleam of amusement in his eyes, and she shook her head.

'I'm sorry.'

She realised she sounded curiously breathless, and the long fingers that curved about her waist, pressed lightly into her yielding flesh for a moment, momentarily putting her at a loss. It was perhaps his way of putting her in her place, but it was stunningly affecting and brought a racing urgency to her heartbeat as they came to the end of the narrow track where the carriage waited. Without for a moment realising how appealing her expression was, she looked up into his face again, but kept her eyes concealed by her lashes.

'Hmm?' he murmured, questioning her appeal, and Francesca shook her head.

'Couldn't you go on calling me Francesca?' she asked.

Antonio set her on her feet and stood looking down at her for a second before he replied; then a faintly sardonic smile touched his mouth briefly and brought colour to her cheeks. 'Why not?' he said. 'You are, after all, very little older than my son.'

Francesca felt as if he had slapped her, although she knew she was probably being too sensitive. Turning so quickly that she winced, she put a foot on the step up into the carriage. Antonio placed both hands on her waist, the long fingers almost meeting as he half lifted her, and when she was settled in the seat she looked directly at him, for his eyes were almost on a level with her own.

He stood in the opening with one booted foot on the step and met her gaze steadily, then he half smiled and lightly touched her cheek with the backs of his fingers. 'I hope this will not discourage you from riding again,' he said. 'Will it, Francesca?'

His slight accent gave her name a much more attractive sound, and for a moment Francesca felt the most curious flutter up and down her spine as he stood there looking at her. Then she remembered what might be in store for Andrés and became anxious again. He no longer carried the quirt, the man leading the horses had taken charge of it while Antonio carried her, but she could remember vividly how that sudden vicious blow had stripped the bark from a tree and she shook her head.

'You won't——' she saw him frown at her curiously and hurried on, not very sure how to say it. 'Andrés,' she said, 'I—I hate any form of cruelty.'

He tilted back his head so that he looked at her down a long autocratic nose for a moment. 'And you believe me capable of any kind of cruelty, eh, Francesca?'

He spoke so quietly, but it was clear that he resented what he saw as her opinion of him, and Francesca sought to put matters right as well as she could. 'I think—I mean, I know that Andrés was making a gesture when he—did what he did. What I'm trying to say is that he saw it as a gesture against me, not just to hurt the animal. You could look at it as a—a move against me, and not blame him so much.'

Antonio regarded her for a moment with narrowed eyes, then he shook his head, as if her reasoning was beyond him. 'And you do not think I would punish him for that?' he asked, very, very quietly.

Francesca's head was spinning and it had nothing to do with her fall, she knew quite well. This man could affect her as no man ever had before. But because of what Andrés had suggested, she shied away from her own reactions, even

while her very feminine senses responded in a way she
could do nothing about.

'I—I don't want anyone punished—not like that, because
of me,' she murmured huskily. 'Please!'

The mare between the shafts stirred impatiently, and the
old driver was plainly waiting to let her move off, waiting
only for permission. Antonio still stood beside the open
doorway with one foot on the step and watching with a disturbingly speculative smile in his eyes. Dropping his raised
foot on to the ground, he stepped back but left his hands
on the carriage sides.

'I hope that my son appreciates the appealing advocate
he has,' he said. 'I shall see that he does!'

He gave a signal to the driver and stepped back as the
carriage started up, and painful as it was Francesca turned
in her seat and looked back at him. He did not appear to
see her, for he was already getting back into the saddle
again, but to Francesca his words could be interpreted in
only one way and she was smiling as she sat back, nursing
her broken arm. She had not had much hope of influencing
him when she made her appeal, but apparently she had
been more successful than she dared hope, and that was
satisfaction enough.

Doctor Juarez had obligingly flown over from San Juan, as
Antonio had said he would, but only when he arrived did
Francesca learn that the two men were lifelong friends. In
the event, the injury to her arm was pronounced merely a
simple fracture, and once it was properly set and a pain-
killing injection adminstered Francesca felt very much
more comfortable.

Cecilia Morales stayed with her throughout, but Francesca could not help noticing how often she cast an anxious
glance at the door. Antonio had met the doctor's helicopter
and ridden back to the house with him, then ostensibly

gone back to estate business. But quite clearly his mother was not convinced that that was his only reason for going off again and she probably believed he had gone in search of his son. Antonio had given her a brief run-down on what had happened and had left his feelings in little doubt, and almost certainly Cecilia Morales feared what he might do when he saw Andrés.

The doctor's parting warning about resting was hardly necessary, for Francesca had seldom felt less like being active, although she acknowledged that she had been incredibly lucky to escape as lightly as she had. It was when the doctor had departed and she sat alone with Señora Morales that she again noticed the older woman's concern and her frequent glances at the door. She began to wonder if her appeal on Andrés' behalf had been as successful as she had first thought, but prayed it had.

'You're worried about Andrés?' she ventured after a few moments, and Señora Morales looked across at her anxiously.

'I am concerned about what Tonio will do,' she admitted frankly. 'To have treated one of the horses so cruelly is enough, but it is something much more serious in this instance, and could have been even worse.' She broke off, shaking her head and obviously very troubled, so that Francesca sought to give her a little reassurance if it was possible, whatever doubts she had herself.

She felt strangely lethargic after the injection, but she did her best to smile at the woman sitting opposite to her. 'I—I tried to make Anotonio see that this was aimed at me rather than at one of his horses,' she said with a slow smile, 'and I think—I tried to persuade him not to take too strong action. I think I might have been successful—I hope so.'

It was obvious that Cecilia Morales did not quite follow her motives, Francesca was not quite sure she understood them herself, but the look in the older woman's eyes was a little less anxious, she thought, and it was worth it to have achieved that. She liked Cecilia Morales, whatever her shortcomings, and she did not like to see her so concerned.

'You spoke to him about this—this thing that Andrés did?'

Francesca nodded, wondering if her intervention would be appreciated for its true motive. 'I couldn't—I mean, I just couldn't face the idea of Antonio doing—what he threatened he would.' She recalled again the violence of the blow that had stripped the bark from a tree trunk, and shuddered. 'I told him that I hated cruelty for any reason, and I think—I'm almost sure he won't do anything to Andrés, not physically anyway.'

Cecilia Morales' faded dark eyes looked at her in mingled astonishment and approbation. '*Querida chica,*' she said softly, 'what a courageous and lovely child you are! But of course Tonio will do as you asked!'

Such extravagant praise was unexpected and brought colour to Francesca's cheeks, but she wished she was more confident of her own influence at the moment. 'I hoped it might make him stop and think at least,' she said with a half rueful smile.

'Oh, but of course——' Cecilia began, then broke off when one of the house servants came in to announce that there was a telephone call for her in the small *salón*; a room that Antonio quite often used as an office.

Shrugging apologetically, she went to answer it, and Francesca took advantage of her absence to lean back in her chair and close her eyes for a few moments. The injection she had been given made her feel rather sleepy and relaxed, and if her companion was going to be engaged on the telephone for a while—— She opened her eyes again quickly when the door of the *salón* opened and Antonio came in, darkbrowed and obviously annoyed and yet curiously anxious too, so that Francesca's senses were immediately alert.

He looked around the room, apparently seeking his mother, and Francesca sat up in her chair, affected by his mood without quite knowing why; he barely glanced at her. 'Madre?' he asked, using the Spanish automatically, she supposed.

'There was a telephone call for her, she went along to the little *salón*.'

He nodded, almost as if he barely heard her, then broke his silence with a sudden and obvious oath in Spanish. 'I cannot find him!'

Francesca almost held her breath while she watched his face and had no need to ask to whom he referred. The tight hard line of his mouth and the shadowy darkness of blue eyes, bright with something other than anger, seemed to suggest suppressed violence and she shivered.

Then she slid to the edge of her chair, ignoring the stiffness of her bruised body that even pain-killers had failed to subdue entirely, for something about him touched her senses and made her heart rap hard and fast suddenly. 'Do you—do you mean he's hiding somewhere?' He would, she thought. Andrés must know that this time he had gone beyond a boyishly malicious prank, but Francesca felt sorry because Antonio had apparently not yielded to her pleas after all and both her words and her tone conveyed her disappointment. 'You went looking for him,' she said.

'Yes, I went looking for him!' Antonio agreed harshly. 'But not with any ideas of thrashing him as he deserves; I thought you realised how successfully you had pleaded for him, Francesca! He had work to do this morning and he has not yet even begun it, *that* is why I went looking for him!'

Francesca's emotions were so tangled that it was difficult for her to know just how she felt. Certainly it afforded her the most incredible satisfaction to be told that he had been influenced by her after all, but she felt anxiety too, because he could not find his son and it obviously worried him. Also, quite inexplicably, she was furious with Andrés more for making so much trouble for his father than for what he had done to her.

'I'm sorry,' she said. 'But he can't have gone very far, surely, can he? I mean, the island isn't all that big that he could hide himself for very long.'

'I know every inch of this island, and every hiding place there is,' Antonio told her with brooding quietness, 'and I have searched every one of them.' Turning swiftly when the door opened once more, he looked at the expression on his mother's face and frowned. 'Madre? *Qué pasa?*'

Cecilia Morales smiled, not a very successful smile it was true, and held her plump beringed hands in front of her as she seated herself once more. 'Andrés is in San Juan,' she said, and Francesca caught the sound of Antonio's indrawn breath. 'It was Julio Juarez on the telephone to let us know that when he agreed to take Andrés with him he did not know that we were unaware of his going.'

'He is still in San Juan?'

Cecilia Morales looked vaguely apologetic and spread her hands helplessly. 'I know only that he landed in Julio's helicopter and that Julio then discovered that he had said nothing to you or to anyone about going away; he hopes that you will understand his part in it.' She looked at her son anxiously, watching his dark face as she spoke. 'Tonio, you will go, *sí?* If you were to go to San Juan and speak with Andrés——'

'Beg him to come back? *No, mi madre, no!*'

Antonio's voice rasped harshly, and somehow his stubbornness and his pride corroded a little of Francesca's sympathy. He wanted Andrés back more than anyone did, but he would not yield sufficiently to go and explain to his son that he did not intend to do as he had threatened, whatever he had done to deserve it.

'He is what Francesca would say—calling my bluff. He

has threatened this on more than one occasion, and he thinks to soften my heart by making me think he has gone for good! No, I will not go!'

Cecilia was looking at him in blank despair and Francesca could not understand his blindness in not seeing the result of his obstinacy. 'Tonio, you must ask him to come home, *mi hijo*!'

'No!' His jaw was set and his brows drawn fiercely, and Francesca saw no chance of him yielding. 'If he wishes to come back, then he must do so without my persuasion!'

'But you *want* him back,' said Francesca, unable to remain silent any longer, 'Why *won't* you ask him?'

He turned on her so fiercely that she heard her own heart thud in a brief moment of panic as he held her gaze. 'Because I do not plead,' he told her in a flat, inflexible voice. 'Not with *anyone*, Miss Dale!'

He turned and was gone, banging the door behind him and leaving a still small silence in the big room. Despite the injection that should have tranquillised her, Francesca felt she had never been more frustrated and annoyed with anyone in her life. How any man could be so stubborn and stiff-necked when his son was concerned, she could not think, especially when she knew so well that he set such store by Andrés carrying on the old tradition.

She was flushed and irritable and her head ached as she sat there glaring at the *salon* door, and she was aware of Cecilia Morales watching her anxiously. 'He will not plead,' Cecilia said in a soft resigned voice. 'It is not Tonio's way, Francesca.'

'Then he deserves to lose his son!' Francesca declared firmly.

Cecilia was shaking her head, her dark and faded eyes gentle as she watched her. 'You do not mean that, child,' she said in her soft voice, and Francesca did not even attempt to deny it.

CHAPTER FOUR

IT had become increasingly obvious during the past few weeks that, despite a determined silence on the subject, Antonio was troubled by Andrés' continued absence, and his grandmother was quite openly concerned. He had, it transpired, managed to hastily gather together all the cash he could find before absconding aboard Doctor Juarez's helicopter, as well as pack a few clothes. It had been done in frantic haste and in the threatening shadow of his father's wrath, but he had been astute enough to make sure he was not without funds and a change of clothes.

It seemed to Francesca that her own relationship with Antonio had mellowed considerably, although there was still an air of reserve in his dealings with her. Being left-handed she could write, if little else, and he had patiently taught her the Spanish headings in some of the more straightforward account books, so that she kept herself occupied with those for a few hours each day, under his occasional surveillance.

Whenever he was bent over her as they studied the books together, Francesca was made aware of how easily that lean, masculine body could arouse her to a response—a response that she did her best to subdue, though rarely successfully. Antonio was often on her mind too, even when he was not actually with her, and realising it was more disturbing than she cared to admit.

'How is he managing to live?'

Francesca brought herself rapidly back to reality, for Cecilia was again speculating on the welfare of her grandson. Quite frankly Francesca was not unduly concerned

71

about how Andrés was faring, for he was a born survivor in her estimation, and unlikely to come to very much harm whatever he was doing. What she did resent was the effect that his absence was having on his family, and inwardly she condemned him as selfish and thoughtless.

Admittedly he had telephoned his grandmother one day, but only to let her know that he was still in the islands. He had not said exactly where he was, nor what he was doing, nor apparently had he asked after his father, and Francesca found it hard not to sympathise with Antonio, whatever his shortcomings. 'I don't think you need worry too much about Andrés,' she told his grandmother. 'He's eighteen and quite capable of looking after himself.'

For all her assurances, the older woman still frowned unhappily, and Francesca guessed she would be inconsolable until her precious grandson came back. 'I worry because he is not like Antonio,' she confessed, and sought to explain when she caught Francesca's enquiring eye. 'Andrés has spent many years in Madrid and he has family and friends there. He is not an island man like Tonio, and I have always feared that something like this would happen. It is why I persuaded Tonio not to send him to university there, for fear he would never come home again.'

'And he knows just how afraid you are of his not coming home again,' Francesca told her. She could remember Andrés' mocking remark about it being the fact that his father believed he would go away that gave him the upper hand. The fact that he was now putting his theory to the test not only appalled her, but made her dislike Andrés more than ever. 'He told me himself,' she went on, 'that he could always blackmail Antonio by threatening to leave.'

'Ah, Francesca, no!' Cecilia's protest suggested that she was shocked by what she heard, and yet Francesca believed that she must have had some inkling.

'I'm sorry,' said Francesca, because it had so clearly done

little to soothe the old lady's fears. 'Quite honestly, Señora Morales, I think Andrés is simply—what we call at home, trying it on. I think he's staying away to prove that he means what he says, but really he's waiting for Antonio to ask him to come home.'

'And Tonio never will,' said Cecilia Morales, resigned, it seemed, to the fact of her son's obstinacy. She sighed and shook her head. 'My poor Francisco always said that those two were like two warring tribes and that it was a miracle that they could both live on so small an island together without killing each other.'

'My grandfather said that?'

In talking about her grandfather, Francesca saw the chance of a respite from the subject of Andrés, and she leaned forward in her chair enquiringly. Cecilia smiled and it was obvious that she was not averse to talking about Francis Dale, although they had so far said little about him. Knowing Antonio's tetchiness on the subject, Francesca had been chary of mentioning him.

'He was a very observant man,' Cecilia told her, 'though a little prone to exaggeration where Andrés and Tonio were concerned. He never quite understood them, you see, they were so very different from him, and I believe he always saw them as—crazy foreigners, yes?'

It was obviously a quote that had amused her at the time of its origin, and Francesca smiled in response. 'It's strange,' she mused, 'but I don't even know what he looked like. All the time he and Daddy were corresponding, he never sent a photograph, and there were none around that I saw.'

It was plain from her expression that Cecilia Morales had enjoyed the years with Francis Dale, and her eyes had a misty softness when she spoke of him. 'You would have loved him,' she said, 'and he would certainly have loved you, Francesca. He was a man with such an—an appetite for love, and so handsome and charming too.'

'You knew him very well, of course,' Francesca ventured, 'living with him for all those years. I mean——'

'I understand what you mean, Francesca.' Soft plump fingers plucked at the skirt of her dress and for the moment her eyes were downcast and her voice so quiet, it was almost as if she spoke to herself. 'We were together, just as you say. For many years I was your grandfather's mistress, Francesca—does that shock you?'

Francesca recalled her mother's rather acid assessment of the situation and shook her head. She was not shocked, more especially now that she knew Cecilia Morales better, and realised she was the kind of woman who needed the support and guidance of a man. She was not the self-sufficient and pioneering type of woman who could have run the estate alone until her son came of an age to take over, and Francis Dale must have come like the answer to a prayer, particularly so when he had proved willing to have her and her son go on living there.

'No, I'm not shocked,' Francesca assured her with a smile. 'I had an idea there might be something like that.'

'Ah!' Cecilia's fingers continued to smooth and pleat the material of her skirt, but Francesca believed it had been a relief to confess her position to someone intimately concerned with Francis Dale. 'At first it was only for Tonio's sake,' Cecilia went on, 'but later on—— He was a good, kind man, and we truly loved one another in the deepest sense of loving.'

'I'm glad.' To Francesca there was nothing wrong with the relationship, but she recalled Antonio's views of her grandfather and could not resist trying to discover if it had always been as uncomplimentary. 'How did—how did he and Antonio get along?' she asked.

A slight shrug of her shoulders said most of what needed to be said, nevertheless Cecilia Morales followed up their implication, though rather reluctantly, Francesca guessed.

'It was never easy,' she confessed. 'Tonio was almost seven years old when his father died, and he had been born and brought up with the knowledge that one day Tradaro's would be his. He would ride around it with his father from when he was a tiny boy, and he knew every metre of it and loved it. He could not understand how it could then belong to a—a stranger.'

'Poor Tonio!' Without knowing it, her expression softened, and Francesca felt a faint twinge of guilt for the first time for having taken away half his inheritance. For the second time he had had a stranger come along and take from him what he had always believed was his by right of birth. 'I can understand how he felt,' she said.

'Also, you see,' Cecilia went on, 'Francisco did not have the same feeling for Tradaro's, nor did he have the skill or the interest to make it flourish as it had in my husband's time. So that for years, until Tonio was old enough to take over from him, it was—not good, you understand.'

Francesca remembered Antonio's own version of the situation and she smiled ruefully. 'I've heard Antonio's opinion of my grandfather's husbandry,' she said, and Cecilia sighed resignedly.

'Sometimes it was very hard. And when Ana came it was worse, because she too did not understand Tonio's devotion to Tradaro's.'

'Ana?'

'Tonio's wife.'

'Oh yes, of course.' It was strange how she had completely forgotten that Antonio had once had a wife, and more curious still how hearing of her now brought an inexplicable sense of resentment which Francesca did not attempt to understand. 'She—Antonio's wife died very young, didn't she?'

'Only twenty-four years—tragically young.'

'Was it an accident? I mean, did she die here on the island?'

It was perhaps probing too deeply, Francesca thought, but somehow it was irresistible to try and learn about the girl Antonio had once been married to; the girl he had brought there as his bride. But Cecilia's fingers still kept up their restless smoothing motion and she kept her eyes downcast, making it obvious that, even after all this time, the matter of Ana Morales' death was not an easy subject to talk about. It occurred to her that perhaps she had gone too far, but after several moments faded dark eyes lifted to her face and studied her for a moment without betraying what was going on behind them.

'I think that lately you have begun to understand my son a little better, have you not, Francesca?'

Unsure just why the conversation had taken that particular turn, Francesca was cautious. 'We get along better than we did,' she allowed. 'But Antonio isn't an easy man to understand, Señora Morales, and I had a lot working against me from the moment I set foot on the island.'

'A proud man, like his father,' Cecilia Morales told her. 'He is very much like my husband was at that age, when I first came here as his wife. I have told you that the Morales have the tradition of bringing out their brides from the old country; Ana was from Madrid, as I was. She was the daughter of an old friend of one of my brothers, and it was a very suitable match in every way.'

Francesca looked up quickly, only half believing, for such things belonged to a different world from the one she knew. 'You mean it was—organised?' she asked, and Cecilia Morales fluttered her hands defensively.

'These things are not done in your country, I know,' she said, 'and Francisco did not approve at all, but—such matters *are* arranged and they most often work well.'

Francesca, to whom the very idea was frankly appalling, tried to imagine a girl coming from the comparatively sophisticated environment of the Spanish capital to this small island, probably only half willing. And she imagined Antonio as he must have been nearly twenty years ago; just as autocratic, just as fiercely possessive about his precious Tradaro's as he was now. A bride who had probably been as unwelcome as she herself had been, and she sympathised with Ana Morales with all her heart, though somewhere deep in her heart she envied her too.

'Poor girl,' she murmured, and was aware that Cecilia was looking at her more critically now.

'Tonio was a very good match,' she insisted.

'I'm sure he was,' Francesca acknowledged, 'but there wasn't much she could do about it if she didn't happen to like him, was there?'

The older woman's expression changed, as if she had been reminded of things she would rather have forgotten. 'Ana hated the islands,' she said. 'From the moment she arrived here she said so. And she had no time at all for Tonio's involvement with Tradaro's, she did not understand his love of the place and she was restless. They were both very young, of course; Tonio was barely past his eighteenth birthday and Ana only a year older.'

'The age Andrés is now,' Francesca reminded her, and Cecilia Morales nodded.

'He was beginning to take an active part in bringing the estate back to what it had been in his father's time, and Ana was often bored. Even when Andrés was born, less than a year after their marriage, she felt no differently, and I am sorry to say that Tonio seemed unconcerned. He never developed any real affection for her, and they saw very little of one another.'

'She must have been terribly unhappy,' Francesca said, knowing from personal experience just how nullifying Antonio's disapproval could be.

Quite obviously Ana Morales had never before been championed quite so outspokenly, and for a moment

Cecilia looked at her a little strangely, as if taking stock of a new aspect of a familiar situation. 'Perhaps so,' she allowed eventually. 'Perhaps that was the reason she left Tonio.'

Stunned for a moment by the unexpectedness of it, Francesca stared, for it was hard to visualise anyone walking out on Antonio, and her sympathies were suddenly divided. She still pitied Ana Morales' unhappiness, but somehow her emotions were more readily swayed by Antonio's situation even though, by his mother's admission, his neglect had led to the parting.

During the past few weeks she had convinced herself that somewhere behind the feudal autocrat was a very human and vulnerable man who had a great deal to offer the right woman. Obviously Ana Morales had not been the right woman, and for the moment Francesca preferred not to speculate on who might be.

'Ana had met someone, during trips to Santo Domingo,' Cecilia went on, 'and just after Andrés had his fifth birthday his mother went to meet this man with the intention of never coming back. It was by accident that I saw the note she left for Tonio, or I would never have believed it of her. What happened to her seemed almost like an act of vengeance, for the storm came up so quickly and the boat she took was so small——'

'She was drowned?'

Obviously reliving those dark moments again, Cecilia Morales sat with her eyes downcast and her hands restlessly smoothing the light fabric of her dress over her knees. 'Tonio was there when they recovered the body and he brought her back here. Ana knew people off the island who we did not, and there were strangers in the church when she was buried, so that—perhaps he was there also, the man she was to have met. But nothing was ever said of why she took out a boat when there were storm warnings. Pride would never let Tonio tell anyone that his wife had been going to another man when she was drowned. She was impulsive—it happened.'

'That pride of his!' Francesca's voice sounded choked and husky, and there was a suspiciously bright gleam in her eyes.

'It is very precious to him, Francesca,' Cecilia told her, gently reproachful, but Francesca saw it as a flaw when it was carried to extremes.

'More precious than his son?' she asked impulsively. She had not meant to get emotionally involved, but somehow where Antonio was concerned she seemed to get involved whether or not she wanted to. 'Oh, Señora Morales, can't he be made to—yield? For your sake if not for his own! It's only his precious pride that stops him from going and bringing Andrés home, which is what you both want!'

She had never before become so deeply entangled in Morales' affairs, but somehow she seemed to have gone too far now to extricate herself. Cecilia Morales had confided in her, telling her something that Antonio had kept from becoming public knowledge for nearly thirteen years, and the confidence sat heavily on her. She was, she believed, bound more closely than ever to Trader's Cay by the secret she had just learned and also, therefore, to the man concerned.

Tears stood high in Cecilia Morales' eyes as she looked at Francesca, and she made no attempt to hide how anxious she was about her grandson. 'I have prayed that one of them will swallow his pride,' she said, 'and I know them both well enough to see that it will have to be Tonio. Andrés is young and he could be as happy other than here, but Tonio— Francesca, if you would just speak with him.'

'Me?' Francesca's heart began a sudden hard and rapid beat at the unexpected plea. Seemingly her attempt to turn Antonio from the brutal revenge he had threatened had been successful, but this was something else again, and she did not see herself with that much influence. 'I couldn't, Señora Morales,' she said, shaking her head firmly. 'I—why, I wouldn't dare interfere in anything like this, Antonio wouldn't even listen to me.'

'Then I do not know what is to be done.'

Plump shoulders dropped despondently and Francesca felt deeply sorry for her, but helpless to do anything to help. Cecilia Morales was being torn apart by the anxiety of the situation, and on the face of it neither Antonio nor his son were the type of men to make the first move. One thing only gave a glimmer of hope; she knew Antonio to be capable of compassion, and she could perhaps reach him like that.

'If I see the opportunity,' she began cautiously, 'I—I'll try and talk to him, *señora*.' A thin and shivery little laugh fell flatly on the silence, and she shook her head. 'But I honestly don't give much for my chances, even if I manage to pluck up enough courage to mention it to him.'

'Francesca, *querida chica*!' Cecilia said softly, the tears trembling in her eyes, 'I think you will need less courage than you believe!'

It seemed that the opportunity to mention Andrés would never arise, and Francesca could not help but feel thankful in one way, for she had very little chance, she felt, of persuading him a second time. It was actually more than three days before she even had the opportunity to be alone with him, and when it happened she did not immediately think of mentioning Andrés.

Antonio had brought in some receipts for her to check off with the accounts book and, as always happened when he was in such close proximity, it was difficult to think clearly about anything. She had never before met a man who had such a devastating effect on her senses as Antonio Morales, and there seemed to be absolutely nothing she could do about it.

With the receipts in his hand, he bent over her, running an eye down the columns of figures in the book, while Francesca tried hard to control the urgent thudding violence of her heartbeat. Her flesh tingled whenever his arm brushed hers and the slight pressure of his weight as he leaned over her shoulder brought a quivering response from her own body. His warmth and the masculine scent of him filled her senses and deepened her breathing until she could do nothing about the exaggerated rise and fall of her breast.

Her colour was high and she could not blame it on the heat alone, any more than she could the slight trembling of her hands as she sifted through the previous day's receipts without any real knowledge of what she was doing. He turned his head slightly towards her and she felt the warm flutter of his breath when he spoke, brushing across her cheek like a caress.

'I have to congratulate you on your mathematics,' he said, and it was impossible not to turn and look at him, even though she knew he would be much too close for comfort.

His face was so dark to have those brilliant blue eyes, and the fine lines at their corners gave added character to the strong features; adding emphasis to his air of maturity, and the firm confidence of his mouth. Just above his brow where the black hair grew thickest, she now knew that faint touches of silver softened the sable darkness, and that in its way was fascinating too.

'I could do better if my Spanish was better,' she told him apologetically. 'It takes me rather a long time sometimes remembering what everything means, but I'm glad you don't still find me useless.'

He did not rise to the bait and in her heart Francesca was glad he didn't, for the last thing she wanted to do was to bring up their past differences. Instead he continued to sort through the receipts he had in his hand, occasionally ticking one off in the book, and from the tone of his voice he was not really interested in what answer she gave him.

'Do you like doing this work, Francesca?'

She supposed she did quite like doing it, and certainly it had kept her occupied while her arm had been out of action. But if she had a choice, she preferred riding out with him in the mornings, and something in his manner made her suspicious. 'I don't mind it,' she told him, and kept her eyes on the strong, spare profile he presented. 'But I feel as if I'm back where I started.' He glanced up and one brow arched enquiringly. 'I was doing more or less the same kind of thing before I came out here,' she explained, 'and I'm not particularly anxious to keep on doing it now that my arm is out of plaster. As soon as I'm able I'll be back to riding with you in the mornings again.'

Antonio finished what he was doing and carefully closed the book, placing the pile of receipts on the desk, then he straightened up and once more Francesca was reminded of how tall he was when he towered over her. Long legs taut and straight in light trousers, the tops tucked into the short boots he always wore, his stance suggested he was about to be stubborn, or lay down the law about something.

'You weren't thinking I'd be content to stay in the office for good, were you?' she asked.

'It would be useful to me if you were here,' Antonio replied, but Francesca was shaking her head at him even before he had finished saying it.

'No. No way are you going to get rid of me by tucking me away in the office, Antonio! I'll be back on horseback again as soon as my arm is strong enough!'

'*Will* you!'

'You said yourself that you hoped the accident wouldn't discourage me from riding again,' she reminded him, and she saw the faintest of smiles touch his mouth for a moment. 'You would remember that, of course,' he said, as if he regretted her doing so, and Francesca glanced up at him from the corner of her eye.

'You've having second thoughts, I suppose?' she suggested, but found it hard to determine just what was going on behind those oddly inscrutable eyes. 'Are you, Antonio?'

'I have no wish to see you hurt again.' He chose his words carefully, Francesca thought, and could do nothing to stop the sudden more rapid beat of her heart.

'Why should you care?' she asked softly. 'If Andrés had succeeded in breaking my neck, it would have saved you an awful lot of bother, wouldn't it? You could have had Trader's Cay all to yourself and handed it down from father to son as it's always been.'

His eyes were fixed on her steadily, and Francesca felt her skin prickling with anticipation when she got to her feet suddenly and in doing so brushed against him. For a moment her legs felt about to give way under her and she gripped the edge of the desk she had been sitting at, for support.

'And you believe that to achieve it I would wish to see you killed?' Antonio asked. 'Do you really think me such a monster of depravity, Francesca? Is that truly your opinion of me?'

He had moved without her being aware of it, and as she stood with her back to the desk he stood directly in front of her, barring her from going anywhere unless he allowed her to. Blue eyes between thick lashes watched her with an intensity that made her shiver, and when he raised a hand and brushed it down her cheek, her eyelids drooped quite involuntarily at its touch.

'I don't know,' she murmured, and briefly moistened her dry lips with the tip of her tongue. 'I—I don't know you well enough to judge how you feel. It isn't easy to know you, you're so—aloof.'

Antonio's long fingers stroking along her jaw were

feather-light and silenced her into breathlessness. She had not foreseen anything quite like this and she felt she should do something to prevent the next inevitable step, even though her heart cried out for it to go on. He raised her chin, persuading it upward with one finger until her mouth was presented to him, soft and yielding with her lips parted and quivering with anticipation.

When he leaned towards her the warmth of his body touched her lightly, almost teasingly, and the thin material of his shirt and of her dress seemed not to exist; it was as if the fierce heat of his flesh touched hers. His hands moved behind her, drawing her into his arms, and the smooth caress of his palms was slow and persuasive as he coaxed her nearer until she could no longer bear any distance between them and surged forward, her face uplifted.

His mouth hovered, lightly touching her lips, then plunged suddenly and searingly into hers, until nothing seemed to exist but the hot, bruising hardness of his kiss. Her body arched, coaxed to surrender by a hard masculine force there was no denying, and she yielded willingly. It was a feeling she had never known before and her every instinct urged complete abandonment as she put her arms up around his neck and curled her fingers tightly into thick black hair.

When she next became aware of anything other than her own desires, it was of a pair of blue eyes looking down into hers, bright and gleaming with an intensity that made her tremble. Her heart still raced wildly and her emotions were in complete chaos as she looked up at him. She had always known that to be kissed by Antonio would be something more than merely a kiss, but she was unprepared for the complete subjugation of her emotions and the alarming response of her own body.

Somewhere at the back of her stunned mind she recalled a reason for wanting to see Antonio alone; some other reason than this. It was something she had promised Cecilia

Morales to do, she thought hazily, but at the moment she could think only of his mouth on hers and the fierce strength of his arms around her. Something she had to persuade him to do, but she could not think what it was.

'Francesca?'

Softly his voice probed her thoughts and Francesca gazed up at him once more, normality penetrating the unfamiliar haze of passion. There was something she had promised to ask him; to try and persuade him. Then she remembered suddenly, but in remembering was reminded of Andrés' mocking suggestion concerning Trader's Cay. He might be tempted to marry you, then he could gain complete control of Tradaro's; wasn't that what Andrés had said?

Francesca shook her head, the excitement of his nearness cooled suddenly by lurking suspicion, and she reached down to clasp the tanned arms that rested at her waist, desperately trying to force them away, to release herself from that dangerous bondage. She had so nearly succumbed and she found herself more angry with her own weakness than with him, whatever his motives.

He had a cause and he would fight for it every way he knew how, but her own reaction had been simply feminine weakness and a desire to know more intimately a man who fascinated her as no man ever had before. Free of his hold, she felt oddly chilled and her body trembled as she walked away from him to stand by the window.

'Am I to apologise?'

His voice was quiet, soft even, yet touched by a thread of steel, and as she half turned her head Francesca sought to subdue the instinctive response of her senses. Somehow she managed to convey a light and casual air, one brow arched enquiringly. 'Do you usually apologise when you kiss a girl?' she asked, and flinched when she recognised an oath.

'Forgive me,' said Antonio in a flat hard voice. 'I forget

that the English attach much less importance to such—incidents.'

'Tonio!' She called out swiftly because she had heard him turn and start across to the door, and her eyes showed just how tangled her emotions were when she looked at him. It was hard, much harder even than she had anticipated when she promised Cecilia to try and persuade him, and it was not the time; not now. She stood the harsh, narrow intensity of his gaze for several seconds before giving way before it, then she shook her head. 'It—it doesn't matter,' she whispered.

He waited for a moment longer and Francesca wondered what was going on behind those bright, unfriendly eyes, then he turned again and went out, closing the door behind him very carefully. She had not even got as far as asking him about Andrés, Francesca thought as she stood by the window and gazed at the door, but it was not for that reason she felt such a sense of regret, and brushed her mouth with the backs of her fingers. She did not care if she never saw Andrés again, for if he had not put that niggling suspicion into her head, those few minutes with Antonio might have had a very different outcome.

Francesca welcomed the unexpected arrival of Doctor Juarez the following morning for several reasons. For one thing because she liked the man who had been a friend of Antonio's for a number of years, and also because by inviting them to his home for the day he offered not only Francesca's first opportunity to leave the island since she arrived, but the chance of a few hours' respite from the increasingly oppressive atmosphere of Trader's Cay.

The chance of a helicopter flight intrigued Francesca too, and she was not sure whether or not she was disappointed by Cecilia Morales' refusal to accompany them. She had declined with thanks while urging Francesca to go with

Antonio and enjoy herself, giving the reason that she was not very fond of flying. In fact Francesca suspected it was because she did not want to take the chance of Andrés returning home and finding no one there to welcome him.

So it was that Francesca found herself borne aloft in the transparent bubble of the doctor's helicopter, and looking down on the hazy green shape of Trader's Cay and thinking how small it looked down there in the gleaming expanse of ocean. It looked beautiful too, and she thought she knew exactly why Antonio fought so fiercely to keep it. Looking at him seated beside the doctor in the front of the craft she caught his eye when he turned his head briefly, and she smiled.

'O.K.?' he asked, straight-faced, and she nodded.

It was the only word he said to her during the flight, and it was Doctor Juarez who pointed out various things of interest as they flew over them. It was Doctor Juarez too who helped her down from the aircraft after they set down on a similar expanse of grassland to that at Trader's Cay. 'My wife will be delighted that you came,' the doctor assured her, and beamed her what Francesca took to be an encouraging smile. As an old friend, he probably knew Antonio well enough to know his moods and make allowances for them, even when the present air of reserve was not directed at him personally. Dark friendly eyes caught and held her gaze for a moment. 'A change of company will be good for both of you, eh?'

Francesca merely smiled her agreement, unwilling to admit there was anything untoward in her relationship with Antonio. It was only a short distance from there to the house, and for the moment Francesca was enraptured by the gardens as the doctor led her along a winding path encroached upon on all sides by a riot of flowering shrubs.

'We have not seen Antonio for a very long time,' the doctor confided, 'so that I could almost be grateful to you for needing my services, Miss Dale. Although naturally I would have been happier had you not been injured.'

Side by side, she and Doctor Juarez walked slightly in front with Antonio following a step or two behind, and it was automatic to glance back every so often. 'I'm as fit as a fiddle again now,' she promised, and stretched out her injured arm to demonstrate the extent of its recovery. 'I've told Antonio I shall be riding with him again soon. Not,' she added with a quick glance over her shoulder, 'that I think he views the prospect with very much enthusiasm, but I'll be glad to get about again.'

'Ah, sitting at a desk does not suit you very well,' Doctor Juarez guessed, and smiled at her knowingly. 'You are the outdoor type, eh Miss Dale?'

'Whenever I have the opportunity,' Francesca agreed. 'It isn't very much fun being tucked away in an office all day.'

'Running an estate like Tradaro's has little to do with fun,' Antonio's voice informed her, and she glanced over her shoulder at him, her eyes brightly green and her confidence boosted by the doctor's obviously sympathetic presence.

'If that's how you feel why do you devote so much of your time and energy to it?' she retorted.

'You know the answer!' Antonio declared harshly, and Francesca turned swiftly away, her cheeks bright and warm.

She refused to indulge in open argument with him in the present circumstances, but a brief glance at the doctor revealed his mouth pulled down into a grimace of understanding. It was meant to sympathise with her, and yet by some odd quirk of her nature it served to make her feel oddly defensive on Antonio's behalf.

Perhaps fortunately, they arrived at the house only seconds later, when the path came to a sudden end at a wide paved patio surrounded by tall trees and flowering shrubs. The house was Spanish in style but more modern in conception than the Morales one, and the doctor invited them in with a smile and a flourish of one hand, his extrovert nature making him an ideal host.

'Please come in, Miss Dale; Antonio!'

Following him in, Francesca stepped into a wide cool hall tiled in pale blue and cream and with several doors opening off it. A pleasant, friendly house; less grand than the Morales home perhaps, but a welcoming one. As they walked in Doctor Juarez called out, walking across the hall as he did so and indicating that they should follow him.

'Susana! *Estoy aqui, querida!*'

He grasped a door handle and turned and at the same time someone on the other side of the door did the same, with the result that there was a brief tussle for possession of it until the one inside the room yielded suddenly. It opened to reveal a short, plump young woman who giggled uncontrollably over the incident while Doctor Juarez put an arm around her shoulders and kissed her heartily before turning to their visitors.

'See who is here, *chica!*'

The girl reached out her hands in welcome, and Antonio pulled her from her husband's embrace into his own, kissing her soundly on her mouth. She beamed him a smile when he let her go and her dark eyes glowed warmly with obvious pleasure. 'Tonio,' she said. 'It has been too long!'

'I agree!' He still held her hand and stood smiling at her flushed face, his lower lip pursed in a decidedly sensual appreciation of her prettiness. 'You grow more desirable each time I see you, Susana. My friend Julio is more fortunate than he deserves to be.'

Francesca had never seen Antonio playing the gallant before and it struck her forcibly how many facets there were to his character that she had yet to learn. The bold speculation in his eyes was something she had glimpsed at only briefly before, and he had certainly never smiled at her as warmly as he did at Susana Juarez; a fact that she found herself resenting more than she cared to admit.

Doctor Juarez again drew her back into his embrace and murmured something in Spanish before introducing her to Francesca. Susana Juarez was a little shy but just as friendly and welcoming as her husband, and it would be hard not to like her on sight. So that Francesca was not at all averse when only shortly afterwards the two men went off somewhere together and left them to their own devices.

It was easy to relax in such pleasant company and outside on the patio under the lacy mauve shade of a bougainvillaea, they sat drinking cool lime juice from frosted glasses while they talked. Probably her hostess was curious about her exact standing, and but for the present uncertain climate between her and Antonio Francesca might have been more forthcoming. As it was the subject was skirted around and never actually mentioned until they had been sitting there for some time.

Catching her eye, Susana Juarez smiled. 'I did not know how to expect you to be, Miss Dale,' she confessed, and laughed a little anxiously when Francesca looked curious. 'I had not seen you, of course,' she went on in her strongly accented English. 'And two people describe so different, eh?'

'*Two* people?'

Francesca frowned curiously over who the second could be. 'My husband has told me that you are very beautiful and charming woman, Miss Dale, and I should perhaps disregard the opinion of Andrés Morales, yes?'

Instantly alert and remembering that Andrés had left Trader's Cay with the doctor's unwitting help, Francesca leaned forward in her chair. 'Have you seen Andrés, Señora Juarez?'

Black lashes hid her eyes and Francesca suspected that the girl was having a tussle with her conscience about something. She had some idea what it must be like at Trader's Cay since Andrés absconded, and by mentioning him she hoped in some way to do something to help, but she did not quite know how, apart from hoping Antonio might do something while he was there. Something like that was in her mind, Francesca thought.

'It is from here that Andrés made the telephone call to Tradaro's,' Susana told her, and Francesca's pulse beat urgently hard at her temple. So near and yet so far away, as far as Antonio was concerned, she feared. 'I had hoped that while you were here, perhaps Tonio would——'

'He swears he won't,' said Francesca, and found it hard to keep the bitterness out of her voice. 'But if you know where he is, Señora Juarez, I might be able to do *something*.'

Susana looked uneasy now that there were definite signs of something happening, and Francesca felt a brief twinge of impatience. She was impulsive herself and sometimes she found it hard to sympathise with caution. 'I do not think that I can say where he is living,' Susana told her. 'Andrés does not wish that we should.'

'Oh, please!' Francesca put down her glass and clasped cool persuasive fingers round the girl's arm. 'His grandmother is going out of her mind worrying about him and maybe if Andrés knew how she's worrying about him he might be persuaded to come back. I feel as if I must at least try, and Antonio has already made his stand; he won't plead with anyone!'

Susana was weakening, Francesca could see it, but she was troubled by the consequences, while Francesca could not see them becoming any worse by the fact of her trying to talk Andrés into coming home, 'Miss Dale——'

'Please call me Francesca,' she begged, smiling hopefully. 'If we're going to be fellow plotters, I feel we should be on first-name terms, don't you agree?'

'Plotters?' A little frown drew Susana's brows close. 'If Julio— —'

'He need not know you've told me,' Francesca insisted. 'Please, Susana; if you could only see how worried his grandmother is about him, and with Antonio being so — so pig-headed, somebody must do *something*!'

'But you cannot go alone to the place where Andrés is,' Susana objected. 'It is—*callejuela*, very poor place, you understand?'

'Yes, I understand,' Francesca assured her, 'but I still want to go and try to talk to Andrés. Please, Susana!'

'I am not happy,' said Susana, and obviously meant it. 'I think that you are —impulsive, Francesca, or you would not do this.'

Francesca's grimace admitted it. 'If I wasn't impulsive I wouldn't have come out to Trader's Cay in the first place. I'd have let the lawyers sell my share of it to Antonio and stayed in my nice safe office job in England; saving the money I got for it for a—a trousseau or something.'

'Safer,' she agreed, 'but a lot less exciting! Now please indulge me in this, Susana, and tell me where I can find Andrés. I'm sorry I'm not being as polite as I ought to be about it, and going off when you and your husband have been so very kind in asking me to your home, but you do see how important this is, don't you? I'm happier without Andrés to be quite honest, but both Señora Morales and Antonio want him home again and they'll both be very unhappy until he is.'

'You do this for Señora Morales' sake?' Susana asked, and Francesca eyed her for a moment from below her lashes.

'Yes, of course,' she said.

Susana took a moment or two more to consider, and it was clear that even when she eventually nodded agreement she was not happy about what she was doing. Nevertheless she wrote down an address on a piece of paper that Francesca gave her and handed it over, still frowning, while Francesca tucked it into her handbag.

'I am not happy,' she insisted, and Francesca pulled a face.

'Nor am I, not entirely,' she confessed. 'But I can be just as pigheaded as Antonio Morales when it suits me, and I've made up my mind to bring this particular impasse to an end.' She glanced over her shoulder as she got to her feet, and clutched her handbag tightly. There was a faint note of hysteria in her laugh as she turned to go. 'I'm sure you're quite convinced the English are crazy, aren't you? But keep your fingers crossed for me, please, Susana; I shall need it when Antonio finds out where I've gone and why!'

CHAPTER FIVE

IT was a small, ugly house, barely more than a shack, when Francesca found it, and even the sight of it made her uneasy. There were too many of the same small, cramped buildings in too little space, mouldering under the sun, and too many children lurking around doorways and the corners of alleys and narrow streets, watching with dark suspicious eyes. Recognising a stranger and suspicious, after the manner of their kind, they followed her every move.

She should not have come, Francesca acknowledged the fact as she went deeper into this teeming jungle of shacks and unpaved streets, but having come so far only fear of her life would make her retreat now. If Andrés was somewhere in this hot, sordid backwater she meant to find him, for otherwise she had risked Antonio's wrath for nothing.

Yet again she checked the address on the piece of paper

she held then, taking a deep breath, raised a hand and knocked. '*Sí, quién es?*'

It was Andrés' voice, she felt almost certain, but Francesca felt it best to make certain, taking account of her surroundings. 'Andrés Morales?'

'*Sí! Quién es, qué desea Ud?*'

Francesca noticed then that the door was ajar and when she placed a cautious hand on it it opened further, giving her a sight of the room beyond. Andrés came out of the shadows, his dark eyes narrowed against the intruding sun, and running a hand through the uncombed mass of thick black hair that fell over his forehead.

'*Madre mia!*' he breathed hoarsely when he recognised her. 'Señorita Dale!' Pushing himself past her he peered out into the street, turning his head in both directions. 'You came here alone? Is my father not with you?'

Francesca shook her head. She realised she was shaking like a leaf and she did not want Andrés to realise it too, so she clasped her handbag tightly in both hands. 'You know he wouldn't come, Andrés,' she said huskily. 'but I—I have to talk to you; just for a few minutes. If you'll let me.'

He did not question the source of her information; how she had been able to find him, but he was as nervous as she was herself, Francesca felt almost certain of it. 'You wish me to invite you into my room?' he asked, and his eyes taunted her. 'Surely not, Miss Dale!'

'Andrés, please!' Nervousness sharpened her voice and its effect was instantly noticeable. As she suspected, Andrés was very much less confident than he seemed and his vulnerability was much more obvious suddenly. He was like a schoolboy who had gone too far with an act of defiance but did not know how to turn back without losing face. 'I don't have to come inside to say what I have to say,' she told him, 'but I hope you'll hear me out, and believe I'm telling you the truth.'

'Say what you will, by all means, *señorita*,' he told her. 'Although I cannot believe that you are here with the approval of my father.'

'He doesn't know I've come to see you,' Francesca allowed, 'but I was—I *am* concerned for Señora Morales.' She saw the quick look of alarm that sprang into his eyes, and hastened to go on. 'Your grandmother is very unhappy; she worries about you all the time, and the longer you stay away the worse it is for her. For her sake I wish you'd give up this—this battle of wills with your father and come home, Andrés.'

Andrés said nothing for a moment, but his lower lip was thrust out and he looked so very much like Antonio that Francesca was perhaps more affected than she might otherwise have been. 'He would not ask me to come back,' he said after a second or two, and Francesca recognised the note of wistfulness when he said it.

Impulsively she reached out and placed a hand on his arm, her eyes fixed appealing on his face. 'It's because he's too proud to give in that I'm here, Andrés,' she told him. 'But he wants you home just as much as your grandmother does, I promise you that.'

Slowly the dark eyes roved over her slightly flushed face and came to rest on her mouth. 'On whose behalf do you plead most earnestly, *señorita*?' he asked. 'My grandmother's —or my father's?'

'On both!' Francesca insisted, and thought she detected a chink in his adamant stubbornness. 'And on my own as well, Andrés.'

'Ah, no! That I cannot believe!' He rubbed the back of one hand across his mouth and his head was bent so that he looked upward at her from below drawn brows. 'I heard— one of the hands said that you were seriously hurt when you were thrown.'

'And that's why you ran away?'

'That is why I left,' Andrés corrected her with dignity.
'My father would have punished me without doubt for
what I did, and I thought it more prudent to leave with
Doctor Juarez.'

Francesca's left hand went instinctively to her almost
healed arm. 'I broke an arm and suffered some bad bruising,'
she told him. 'Nothing like as severe as it could have been.'

'I am sorry for your injuries.'

He sounded as if he meant it, although Francesca suspected that he would probably do something similar again if
he thought it would help to dislodge her from Trader's
Cay. Still, she was too close to achieving her object now to
let anything stop her, and time was passing. Before long
Antonio would discover where she had gone and, while she
knew he would never demean himself to come chasing after
her, she would be thankful to leave that depressing district
and return to the Juarez home.

'I'll forgive you anything if you'll just give up this waiting
game with your father and come home,' she promised.

Andrés raised his head and again she was reminded of
Antonio when he looked at her down the length of an autocratic nose in a way that told her she was taking too much
for granted. 'I do not think my father will be so readily
appeased, Miss Dale,' he told her. Obviously he had recovered some of his confidence now that she had made it
clear how desperately he was missed at Trader's Cay. 'I too
have my pride,' he went on, 'and I do not intend to be
punished like a schoolboy.'

'You won't be——'

'You cannot presume to speak for my father, Miss Dale,
no matter how much influence you believe you have over
him!' It was true, Francesca had to allow, and Andrés drew
himself up, running his fingers through the ungroomed mass
of his hair. 'I will consider what you have told me and—
decide,' he said.

He was so much a Morales, even here in this narrow slum street, that it was hard to believe in the vulnerable youth she had glimpsed only a few minutes before, and she moistened her lips anxiously when she looked at him. 'Please decide soon, Andrés,' she said. 'Señora Morales——'

'I will telephone my grandmother when I have decided,' Andrés interrupted coolly. 'And now I advise you to leave, Miss Dale.' He glanced across the mean street to where a stout dark woman with a baby on her hip watched from a doorway with frank curiosity. 'You make these people suspicious with your strange colouring and fine clothes, and you do not belong here.'

'Do you?' she asked, and darted a quick nervous glance over her shoulder. Turning back, she found the door already closing again. 'Andrés!'

But the door was firmly closed against her and she had little option but to accept its message. Maybe she had managed to get through to him, but Andrés was as single-minded and just as sensitive to his own pride, as his father was, and she now had to return empty-handed and face Antonio's disapproval. She had little doubt that he would have been angry about her going, whatever the outcome, but a positive response would have helped.

Making her way back along the hot dusty street she walked as quickly as she could without appearing to flee from an environment that was unnervingly alien, and dark eyes followed her every foot of the way. Made bolder by her withdrawal, a handful of boys, shoeless and ragged, chanted something in their own tongue, then laughed; confident that she could not understand the words, but equally sure she understood the meaning.

Francesca kept her eyes forward and tried to ignore them, but they were at her heels and she felt a rising sense of panic that grew in pitch with their boldness, until she was shaking like a leaf. She turned a corner, but the street was little different, and she was aware that the narrow mouths of alleys disgorged more urchins, while those who had followed her thus far sidled back to their own defined territory.

She hurried between the rows of shacks and they followed, murmuring in their own tongue and occasionally sending up explosions of laughter that mocked her obvious nervousness. Naked brown soles slip-slapped on the uneven stones, softly menacing and just out of sight unless she turned her head, which she was loath to do. Only occasionally from the corner of her eye did she catch sight of a thin childish foot skipping back after coming just that little bit too close.

Around another corner and the street became slightly wider and the houses less ramshackle, and a taxi-cab was pulled up at the far end of it letting off a passenger. No taxi driver would venture too far into such a district, she guessed, and rued her own rashness in doing so. The passenger leaned into the window of the cab and handed over some money, receiving a brief salute in return, and the moment the passenger straightened up, Francesca recognised him.

'Antonio!'

When he turned it was as if in answer to her whispered murmur of relief, yet he was much too far away to have heard it, and she half turned her head at the faint sound of scuttling feet behind her. When she looked back over her shoulder the ragged army of urchins who had pursued her were no longer there, but swallowed up in the labyrinth of alleyways.

She saw Antonio recognise her, then caught her breath in sudden alarm when he seemed to be turning away from her. She started to run, heedless of the impression it might give, more afraid of his leaving than she had been of the unspoken threat that had followed her from the shanty-town slums. But he went no further than the edge of the footpath, then she saw him raise an arm and signal, and realised he was recalling the taxi-cab he had just dismissed.

Even so Francesca did not slow down, but kept on running on legs that felt increasingly as if they were going to collapse under her. The taxi must have made a U-turn and it stood waiting with with the rear door open and Antonio beside it, one hand on the handle, dark and lowering as a storm cloud as she came racing up.

'Antonio— —' she began, but he wasted no words.

Iron-hard fingers gripped her arm and thrust her into the back seat of the vehicle, forcing her right across the width of it until she was brought up short against the far side, then he climbed in beside her. He gave the driver an order in Spanish, and the taxi pulled away while Francesca still coped with an ache in her side from running so fast, and for the moment neither of them said anything.

He looked furiously angry and the profile he presented offered little encouragement. Nevertheless when she felt she had breath enough, Francesca ventured a question, looking at the strong arrogant face as she did so. 'Antonio, weren't you—aren't you going to see Andrés?'

'I came in search of you because Susana was afraid for your safety, that is all.'

His tone was as hard and unrelenting as his features, but even so her heart gave a flutter of response at the idea of his coming to find her, though she wished she could persuade him to go and see Andrés now that he was there. 'You could,' she ventured, 'you're so close— —'

'*Condenación!*' Antonio swore harshly. 'Will you cease to plague me?'

'I only thought that as I'd seen him and— —'

'You have interfered in a matter that does not concern you, so do not expect me to thank you for it, Francesca!' Again he cut across what she was saying, his voice harsh and forbidding, like the look on his face. 'You should know me well enough by this time to know that I do not tolerate anyone meddling in my affairs!'

He spoke in a low voice despite his anger, so that the driver was unlikely to hear what he was saying, but there was no mistaking the passionate fury of it, and Francesca despaired of ever making him understand her motive. Glancing at the back of the driver's head, she too spoke in a low voice and her hands were tightly clenched on her lap as she pressed on with her cause.

'I know how worried Señora Morales is,' she told him. 'She's half out of her mind worrying about Andrés, and you won't do anything about it! I know you're as anxious as she is to have him back——'

'You assume to know a great deal!' Antonio interrupted shortly.

'I know you're—pigheaded and—and obstinate——'

'That is enough! My feelings for my son are my own concern!'

'You *know* you want him to come home!' Her disappointment with Andrés added to her frustration and she looked at him despairingly. 'Oh, you're so unbending! If only you'd been with me I'm certain Andrés would have made up his mind there and then to come home, instead of dithering about it! You're as bad as one another!'

Antonio turned swiftly and his eyes were narrowed between their thick lashes while he swept his gaze over her flushed face for a moment before he asked, 'He has said he will return to Tradaro's?'

Clutching her hands tightly together on the clasp of her bag, Francesca was half decided on a lie. 'It's—it's possible,' she said, not meaning to deceive only to encourage. 'He says he'll let his grandmother know when he makes up his mind.'

'*Madre de Dios!*' Antonio swore. 'How dare he!'

From the corner of her eye Francesca studied his face and

she noted the lines that traced the shape of his mouth and the shadows that lay beneath the blue eyes. He was every bit as anxious as his mother was to have Andrés home again, but he was still not prepared to swallow his pride and ask him. Acting on impulse, as she so often did, Francesca placed a hand on his arm, pressing her fingers into the taut muscles beneath a tailored cream jacket.

'He's proud and a little wary of losing face, Tonio,' she murmured in a softly husky voice. 'Like you, he doesn't give in easily, and he isn't sure how to in this case. I *might* have persuaded him, I don't know, but you could if you just went and saw him.'

She looked at him from below her lashes, and her eyes were slightly misty because her emotions were more involved than she anticipated. He did not turn his head again, but nor did he shake off her persuasive hand, and his voice was less harsh when he answered her, as if her appeal had some effect.

'I can well believe that you have persuaded him,' he said, 'and since you say he is making his own decision on the strength of what you have said to him, then I shall let him make it.' He turned and looked at her and it was difficult to say what might be going on behind the deep, inscrutable look in his eyes. 'As for you, *mi muchacha*, if you attempt once more to teach me how to handle my son I shall take steps to put you very firmly in your place. Do I make myself clear?'

'But I——'

'I know that you mean well,' Antonio went on smoothly, just as if she had not spoken, 'otherwise I would have done something about it before this. But I will not tolerate any further interference in family affairs, Francesca. I happen to know Andrés very well; who better since you say he is like me? But I will no longer tolerate his particular type of emotional blackmail.' He looked round at her, his gaze on her mouth in a look that reminded her irresistibly of the way he had kissed her, so that she kept her eyes downcast. 'Nor will I be weakened by the soft words of a pretty girl,' he went on, speaking much more gently, 'no matter how appealing she may be. Do you understand me?'

'Perfectly!' Francesca assured him with breathless sarcasm and a swift upwards glance.

'Good!' He appeared not to notice the sarcasm and took the assurance at face value. 'Then it remains only for you to make your apologies to Julio and Susana, and we can take up where we left off and begin to enjoy ourselves.'

Francesca felt she had taken quite enough for the moment without being awarded a metaphorical pat on the head, and she glared at him reproachfully. 'I'll enjoy myself more if you'd stop talking to me as if I was a naughty little girl!' she informed him. 'You're not *my* father, Antonio!'

He turned his head and looked at her for a long, wordless moment before he replied, and something she saw in the depths of his eyes brought hot, bright colour to her cheeks. 'For which I thank heaven,' he assured her piously. 'I would find you much more difficult to deal with even than Andrés!'

'Tonio——'

'Be quiet,' Antonio told her firmly, 'I will not argue with you.'

The barely concealed challenge brought an active response from her senses and there was a warm bright glow in her eyes, while her pulse hammered relentlessly, making her head spin. 'Because you're afraid you'd lose?' she suggested in a throatily husky voice, and Antonio turned his head, surveying her lazily for a moment.

'Because I am certain that I would,' he confessed, then frowned with mock severity when she laughed suddenly.

Francesca thought Susana Juarez was a little subdued during lunch, and wondered if her husband had disapproved of her involving herself in his friend's affairs by handing over Andrés' address. She would have been sorry to cause controversy in any case, but the Juarez were such an idyllically happy couple that she hated to think her actions had caused friction between them.

'I feel rather guilty about getting Susana into trouble too,' she said, having apologised for her earlier absence, and catching the doctor's eye she knew she had guessed correctly. 'I shouldn't have inveigled her into giving me the address.'

'I have scolded her, and it is forgotten,' Doctor Juarez assured her, and reached for his wife's hand and kissed it, as if to prove his point.

There was mingled amusement and curiosity in his gaze, and Francesca ignored Antonio's attempt to signal her to silence. 'It was entirely my fault,' she insisted. 'Susana was very reluctant to part with it, but I convinced her that it was for the best and she gave in out of the goodness of her heart.'

'My wife has a very warm heart,' Doctor Juarez assured her solemnly, but a smile warmed his dark eyes when he looked at Francesca. 'But, my dear *señorita*, I am quite certain that you are able to charm anything you wish to know from anyone, if you have made up your mind to do so, eh? If Andrés *does* return to Tradaro's, then I am sure it will be because you have asked him to.'

'Oh, good heavens no, it won't!' Francesca could feel Antonio's gaze on her as she shook her head. 'All I can do is hope I was convincing enough to make him realise how much Señora Morales worries about him. But if he does decide to come home it will be because he's anxious about his grandmother, not to please me. Definitely not to please me!'

'Oh?'

An arched brow questioned the truth of it from Antonio, but he was apparently too busy with his lunch to respond.

The fact that the doctor appeared to be in ignorance regarding the basic cause of her accident came as something of a surprise to Francesca. For while she could understand Antonio not wanting it widely known that his son had been indirectly responsible, it was strange that he had not confided in a close friend.

'Do you not get along well together?' Julio Juarez pressed on, despite a warning glance from his wife. Tact was presumably not the doctor's strong point and could possibly account for his not knowing about Andrés.

'Let's just say that we have our differences,' Francesca told him with a faint smile.

'But who does not? What is it that makes this—difference between you?'

The doctor was apparently irrepressible, but Francesca only reluctantly offered a possible cause, and that only after a vaguely apologetic glance in Antonio's direction. Still he did not look up, and yet she got the impression that he was alert to every exchange, listening without contributing anything himself.

'Who knows?' she asked. 'Maybe it has something to do with the fact that Andrés is a fiery Latin and I'm a fiery redhead—it isn't a very comfortable combination.'

'And yet you do not fight with my friend here,' Doctor Juarez insisted. 'And is the situation not the same?'

He looked around hopefully for an answer, and again Francesca looked across at Antonio to see what his reaction was. Briefly he looked up from his meal and one black brow arched above heavily lidded eyes. 'Do not assume too much, Julio,' he told the doctor quietly.

'*Madre mia!*' Doctor Juarez exclaimed in disbelief. 'What are we coming to? Perhaps, *señorita*,' he said, again turning to Francesca, 'you have someone in England, eh? I will not believe that such a lovely young woman does not have at least one gallant *hombre* in love with her!'

'No one at all, doctor.' Francesca wished the subject could be dropped, for she was finding it increasingly discomfiting. For one thing because that sense of awareness in Antonio was oddly unnerving; he listened, but said nothing, and she had the feeling that he was waiting to hear what she had to say on the subject with more interest than made sense. 'I had several casual boy-friends, ones who took me out sometimes, but no one serious.'

'Hah!' Raised hands despaired of her compatriots' shortcomings in that direction. 'We must try to remedy the situation now that you are in the islands, Miss Dale, and since you do not—hit it off?—with my friend and his son, we must look elsewhere to find you a handsome husband, eh?'

His persistence would have been more irritating if he had not been so likeable, but still Francesca found the subject embarrassing, especially with Antonio sitting across the table from her—not looking at her but listening to every word, she felt sure.

'I'll cope with finding my own husband, thank you, Doctor Juarez,' she told him with a rather strained smile.

'You think a young woman is capable of deciding such an important issue for herself?' Doctor Juarez asked, his eyes twinkling, and Francesca took him up swiftly.

'Oh, perfectly capable, doctor! I'm already alert to the possibility of being loved and married for my share of Trader's Cay rather than for myself!'

It was irresistible when she glanced across the table at Antonio and she noticed that he no longer gave his attention to his meal but watched her steadily through slightly narrowed eyes. She had reminded him as well as herself, she guessed, of those few moments in the study yesterday, and he would know why she had so determinedly broken his hold on her. Nevertheless her pulse quickened and her flesh tingled when she recalled the warm hardness of his

body and the ravishing fierceness of his kiss. She could
almost believe it made being wooed for what she possessed
worthwhile—almost, but not quite.

'Ah, but I cannot believe that in your case it will be so,'
Doctor Juarez insisted gallantly, and again Francesca
replied swiftly and without stopping to think.

'Andrés suggested it was a distinct possibility, my first
day here!'

There was a curious air of stillness about Antonio, and his
hands clenched into fists where they rested on the snowy
tablecloth. In any other situation Francesca believed he
would have tackled her with it unhesitatingly. As it was he
was obliged to sit there and face her across the table, bound
by good manners to be silent, but knowing that she suspected him of trying to seduce her to gain her share of the
island; more, that she had been alerted to the possibility by
his own son.

'I will remember that!' said Antonio, and those were the
last words he said to her on the subject for the rest of their
visit.

Flying back to Trader's Cay the view from the helicopter
was breathtaking and at any other time would have brought
cries of delight from her. But while the sky turned purple
and gold, and the Caribbean a depthless blue, Francesca sat
in the back seat of the craft and gave her attention to
studying the back view of Antonio's dark head.

Arrogant and proud, autocratic and unyielding; all those
terms she had used to describe him since she came to
Trader's Cay, and yet there was something else too. Some
indefinable something that could touch her heart and in
some curious way weakened her resistance to his over-
bearing authority.

As if he was aware of her scrutiny, he half turned his head
as they started the descent on to the familiar stretch of
grassland, and for just a moment the blue eyes held hers, a

slight frown gathering his brows. Then one brow arched upward suddenly in silent query, and she automatically nodded her head, touched again by that inexplicable sense of rapport. Even in his present unapproachable frame of mind he showed concern, questioned her nervousness at landing, and it somehow mellowed the suggestion of aloofness.

It was Antonio who helped her down from the helicopter, while Doctor Juarez remained in the pilot's seat, ready for immediate take-off. 'I have promised to be home by darkness,' he confessed, with a wry grin to excuse his obedience to his wife's wishes. 'The nervousness of women, hah? *Hasta la vista, mis amigos!*'

They waved him off and as Francesca turned away, she glanced at the dark unfathomable face beside her. 'He's nice,' she ventured.

'I think so.'

It was hardly encouraging, and there was something vaguely menacing in the way he paced across the grass strip towards the house; something of the tautness and the suppressed violence of a stalking cat. A few minutes of walking along beside him was enough for Francesca and she sought to make her escape, a small flutter of anticipation making butterfly movements in her stomach.

'I'll run on ahead and let Señora Morales know we're back!'

She spoke quickly and breathlessly and she would have darted off had not Antonio's strong fingers closed around her left wrist. She spun round and found herself pulled towards him until the firm unyielding length of him stopped her short, and her heart was beating so hard that her body shook with its pounding. Raising her eyes to his face was as purely automatic as the nervous darting of her tongue across her lips.

'If you go to seek protection from me, *niña*,' he told her

harshly, 'you have no need! Now that I know you have been warned what to expect of me, I shall not waste time trying to seduce you!'

Francesca felt as if she had been slapped hard, and she stared up at him, too dazed for the moment to take it in. Deep in her heart she admitted that she had never really believed it of him, and yet here he was admitting it quite boldly. It was as if a cold hard weight had settled in the region of her heart, for only now did she realise how close she was to being in love with him. He could so easily have achieved what he set out to do if he had denied it rather than confirmed it, for even with Andrés' warning in mind she had found it all too easy to yield, and if he had persisted she would have weakened, she knew it.

'Antonio——' She hesitated, shaking her head. 'You—you admit that Andrés had grounds for warning me? That you——'

'I admit nothing,' Antonio interrupted shortly. 'But you left no one in any doubt what you believe! You see any attempt to——' His hands made swift and sharply erotic gestures that brought bright colour to her cheeks. 'I am merely giving you my assurance that in future you are quite safe from *my* attentions!'

If she had stopped to consider her reaction in the light of reason, Francesca would have despised herself for trying to appease him. But as it was she responded to an impulsive need to placate him if she could, regardless of the rights of the matter. 'Antonio, I didn't mean that—that I thought you were——'

"Trying to seduce you for your share of Tradaro's?' he asked, abrasively harsh. 'Who else fits the situation you hinted at, Francesca, eh?' His fingers grasped her tightly, holding her arm to the pulsing warmth of his chest so that she could feel the thud of his heartbeat almost as rapid as her own. 'What other man on this island has had the opportunity, the insolence, to kiss you as I did, eh?'

'No one!'

Half indignant, she looked up at him, the colour high in her cheeks and a glinting brightness in her green eyes, and gasped when he thrust her from him suddenly, rubbing her hand over the marks his fingers had left. Anger stirred, but the softness of appeal still lingered in the look she gave him.

'Now you may go and inform Madre that we are back!' he said, and Francesca shook her head slowly.

There was a curious sensation stirring in her that tingled and teased, and brought with it a wild tangle of emotions she did not begin to understand. She moved beside him when he resumed his striding progress across the sward, growing breathless as she tried to keep pace with him. 'Tonio, you don't——'

'*Condenación*, will you go and leave me in peace!' he swore, and Francesca clenched her hands tightly.

She regretted having started this latest dissension, she admitted as much to herself, but when he was in this stubborn uncompromising mood he infuriated her. She tossed back the red hair that proclaimed her fiery temper and hurried to match his lengthening stride.

'If you mean will I go away from Trader's Cay and leave you in sole possession—*never*!' she declared breathlessly. 'The only way you'll get your hands on my half *is* by marrying me, as Andrés said! And *that* isn't even a possibility!'

Antonio swore in Spanish as he strode on towards the house. 'I would as soon be married to a *regañona*!'

Panting and pink-cheeked, Francesca sought to keep pace and at the same time see his face. 'What's that?' she demanded suspiciously.

'A shrew!' She opened her mouth to object, but quite unexpectedly he showed his teeth for a moment in a hard bright smile. 'A little mouse with an inquisitive nose and a sharp bite, *niña*. But it is not impossible to catch, remember that!'

He deliberately lengthened his stride suddenly in an attempt to outpace her and Francesca found herself left behind, unable to compete. But while she slowed her own gait to something less taxing, there was a curious little half-smile on her lips. She resented being dubbed a shrew, but it wasn't that which stayed in the forefront of her mind, it was the idea that those last few words had conveyed a promise as much as a threat; and it was that that made her smile.

CHAPTER SIX

FRANCESCA looked forward to getting back into her routine again, and even the thought of an early start did not spoil her anticipation. She was out of bed and partly dressed when she heard Antonio go past her bedroom door on his way downstairs, and she smiled to herself. She had said nothing to him about resuming her daily ride, but meant to surprise him; the possibility of his not being pleased about it did not yet occur to her.

For the past couple of days, ever since their visit to Doctor Juarez and his wife, the situation between them had been somewhat tense. The possibility of Andrés deciding to return was on all their minds, and Francesca for one hoped he was not going to keep them too long in suspense. But there was also that rather emotional conversation they had had while they walked back to the house, which had left her strangely excited rather than subdued, as she was probably meant to be.

It was difficult to decide whether or not she wanted

Andrés to be swayed by her pleas. For Señora Morales' sake she would like to have him back, and Antonio too, despite his reluctance to admit his feelings, would almost certainly welcome him. For herself, Francesca did not see how things were ever going to be any different from what they had always been between her and Andrés, and for that reason she could wish her mission had failed completely.

She sighed as she made her way downstairs, and felt the sudden hard thud of her heart when she caught a glimpse of Antonio through the *salon* door. It did not occur to her that he was still in the house for any other reason than that his mother had informed him of her intention to join him, and she hurried down the rest of the stairs and across the hall, her eyes smiling and a slight flush in her cheeks.

She hesitated for a moment in the doorway, taking stock of him while he was still unaware of her presence. He stood with his back to her and his hands clasped behind him, a tall and vaguely menacing figure outlined by the arched window and with a background of blue morning sky. The scent of a frangipani that grew near the window filled the cool salon and brought an exotic touch to the formal Spanish room; and in the stillness it was possible to catch an occasional burst of excitable Spanish from the domestic quarters, a warm comfortable sound.

Francesca watched him, and as she did so she experienced a curious tenderness that she was hard put to account for. A feeling that made her want to reach out and touch him, because there was a quite unexpected look of vulnerability about the dark head and the familiar stance. A feeling that must have been almost tangible, for he turned slowly towards her after a moment or two, as if he sensed her there.

The customary swift and explicit survey of her from head to toe was probably automatic. A bold, and curiously possessive scrutiny that took note of every detail of her face and figure, and aroused far too many responses for her comfort. '*Buenos días*, Francesca,' he said, and his use of the Spanish gave her a moment of surprise.

'Good morning, Antonio.' She regarded him with her head to one side and smiled tentatively. 'How did you know I'd be joining you this morning? Did Señora Morales tell you?' Only then did it occur to her that he might *not* have been waiting for her, but had some other reason for delaying his departure, and she squirmed inwardly. 'Are you—I mean, you are waiting for me, aren't you?'

It was almost a plea, because she hated the idea of him thinking she took his attendance for granted, but he nodded and a faint smile twitched at one corner of his mouth. 'Why else would I still be here at this hour of the morning?' he asked. 'Madre told me last night that you had made up your mind to resume your daily routine. I have to admit that I was a little——'

'Put out?' Francesca suggested, quickly defensive because she could well imagine that had been his reaction to the news. 'I can imagine you don't relish the idea of having me trailing along, but I'll soon learn to manage on my own and then you won't have to—to nursemaid me along.'

'I was about to say I was a little surprised, that is all,' Antonio informed her with what struck her as a very untypical tolerance. Again he swept that disturbing gaze over her, tapping the riding whip he carried in the palm of one hand. 'Since you appear to be quite ready, may I now leave and get on with my work?'

'Yes, of course.' She had no intention of being left behind and her look conveyed as much. 'I hope you don't blame me because you're late starting; I didn't expect you to wait for me!'

An arched brow commented on her tone. 'I realise I am under no obligation,' he agreed quietly. 'But if you intend to start the day by quarrelling with me, Francesca, I will leave you and not trouble myself further.'

'Oh no, please! I'm glad you waited, really!'

She spoke up quickly, not even noticing that he had made no actual move to leave, despite his threat, and he inclined his head, indicating that she should precede him across the room. Following close on her heels, he leaned past her to open the outside door, and he smelled warm and fresh, his skin when his arm brushed against hers suggesting that he had not long come from the shower. To Francesca his proximity was as disturbing as it had always been, and she despaired of it ever being any different as she walked with him out into the morning sunshine.

The gardens always seemed especially attractive at that time of day, and she felt oddly alert to everything around her this morning. Happy to be getting back to normal, and looking forward to the morning routine in a way she never had before. They were making their way past the thick riot of shrubs that part-covered the path to the stable when Antonio's voice broke into her thoughts.

'Are you not in rather too much hurry?' he remarked, and she looked up at him curiously. 'Surely it would have been wiser to wait before you try riding again, Francesca.'

'Do you really think so?' she asked.

'Very definitely I think you should! I tried to tell you so just now.'

His vehemence surprised her. She would not have been surprised by advice that she should take things easy for a while, but outright discouragement was unexpected and for a moment she was not quite sure how to react. Her arm was very much better, but if she overdid it sometimes it ached and became stiff, so his opinion made some sense.

'Doctor Juarez said it was O.K.,' she ventured, but Antonio swiftly denied it.

'It is improving. I was there when he said it, Francesca, and there was nothing mentioned of horse-riding. I do not imagine Julio even thought of it.'

It was his motive that puzzled Francesca for the moment. Much as she would like to believe that it was concern for her that moved him, the suspicion that he was trying to rid himself of an unwelcome companion refused to be dismissed. 'Why are you trying to put me off, Antonio?'

He strode along beside her, so obviously containing his long stride to accommodate her, and she sensed him frown over the question. 'Because I do not wish you to overtax your injured arm too soon,' he insisted, then went on quickly before she could say anything. 'If I merely wished to avoid your company, Francesca, I had only to go without you this morning instead of waiting in the *salón* for you to come down.'

'I didn't——' she began, but he cut her short.

'I suspect you did! You have an unfailing belief that I am motivated solely by a desire to make things as uncomfortable as possible for you, and I do not find it very flattering!'

'I *don't*, I honestly don't, Tonio!'

'Then believe that I am concerned only that you do not overtax yourself,' he said, evidently convinced by her assurance.

Francesca's emotions were hopelessly confused at the moment. She had looked forward to riding again and to resuming her early morning routine with him, but at the same time the idea of his being so concerned with her well-being was equally satisfying. And she basked for a moment or two in the warm glow it gave her, as they skirted by a massively overgrown hibiscus that drooped huge blue heads to the ground.

The morning wind blew coolly across her brow and stirred strands of copper red hair, and when she put up both hands to push it back from her face the movement was unwittingly provocative. She realised it only when she became aware that Antonio was watching her, and hastily lowered her arms again, made conscious of the soft rounded shape under the subtle flattery of a fine lawn shirt.

'I was rather looking forward to it,' she confessed in a slightly breathless voice. 'But if you think I shouldn't ride yet, Tonio, then I won't.'

He turned his head and looked down for a moment at her small neat profile with its soft mouth and downcast eyes hidden by shadowing lashes. 'Obedience to my wishes?' he questioned softly. 'This is something new Francesca. The least I expected was outright defiance and the demand that I mind my own business!'

Francesca's eyes were reproachful, like the slight thrust of her bottom lip, as she looked up at him. 'And you were the one who accused me of trying to start the day with a quarrel!' she accused. 'I'm not too pigheaded to take advice, when it makes sense—unlike some people!'

For a moment she was afraid he might rise to the bait, and Francesca really had no wish to quarrel with him, whatever impression she gave. But instead, to her relief, he said nothing, and although she had decided not to ride, she continued with him on round to the stable, waiting while Garcia, the stable-boy, brought out the black mare that Andrés had always been so fond of riding.

Andrés was impressive on horseback, but he lacked his father's more sophisticated arrogance in the saddle, and Antonio was never less than awe-inspiring. Having handed over the animal to its rider, Garcia discreetly drifted away as he always did, and Antonio sat looking down at her, holding the restless mare with the firm gentleness he always showed his animals.

'What will you do, Francesca?' he asked, and she shrugged, feeling somewhat at a loose end now that she had been persuaded against taking her ride.

'Walk down to the sheds, perhaps. I expect you'll be going that way too, won't you? I believe there's a boat due in, isn't there?'

Antonio checked the time. 'Later. But Perez will be taking charge this morning; I have to deal with some trouble in the *aldea*.'

'Oh!' Her disappointment was barely disguised. 'Well, I can help Perez.'

'I think not,' Antonio decreed unhesitatingly. 'I shall instruct Perez that until you are completely recovered I am not allowing you to do anything at all.'

For a moment his arrogance took her breath away. As if he was sole owner and in a position to tell her what she might or might not do! Francesca thought, and looked up at the tall, dominant figure that loomed over her with a challenging glint in her eyes. 'You won't *allow* me——'

'I will not allow you!' he stressed firmly. 'You have already shown yourself sensible in accepting advice, Francesca, please do not insist on being foolish merely for the satisfaction of disobeying me.'

'It's that word allow I dislike,' Francesca informed him. 'It would be more tactful to—*suggest* I don't do anything yet.'

Antonio swore softly in Spanish and from the corner of her eye she noticed that his hands tightened a little on the rein. '*Muy bien*,' he said in a carefully controlled voice. 'Then I *suggest* that you do not do anything too strenuous for the moment, but simply take working slowly.'

Somehow Francesca found those rare and minor mistakes in English oddly endearing, and she smiled faintly, yielding far more willingly than he probably realised. 'I'll take things slowly,' she promised. 'I know you mean it for my own good, Antonio.'

'I am glad that you realise it is!' He held the impatient mare on a tight rein, still curious about what she meant to do. 'Then what will you do with yourself?'

'I might as well have stayed in bed a bit longer,' she told him with a rueful smile. 'But I think I'll walk down to the sheds anyway, and see the green boat come in. I promise, I won't do a thing to help!' she added swiftly, and laughed at his frown because she also saw the dark gleam of amusement in his eyes.

'One thing more,' he warned before he moved off. 'There is warning of a storm, Francesca, so make sure that you are not too far from shelter wherever you go.'

Yet again he concerned himself with her welfare, and it gave Francesca a warm comfortable feeling as she smiled up at him. 'Thank you for the warning—I'll remember not to stray too far.'

He nodded, apparently satisfied that she would do as she said, then he nudged his mount into action and raised a hand in salute as he moved off. '*Hasta luego!*'

Francesca watched him ride off regretfully, for she really had been looking forward to going with him. The decision had been a wise one though, she had to admit, and she followed him out of the yard on foot, taking the main track down to the sheds as she had said she would. It was so different now that the field workers were used to her and, although she did not understand their Spanish, questions about her recovery were easy to understand, and she answered by holding up the arm in question and nodding her head.

The sheds at the end of the pier were a hive of activity, as always when there was a boat in, and she noticed that a gleaming white freighter built with a superstructure as big as a luxury liner, was already stood off out at sea and being loaded. The draft required by the enormous vessel meant that it could not come in to the pier, and the small boats plied back and forth like beetles, loaded to the gunwales on the outward trip with cardboard cartons of green bananas.

Things seemed to be slackening by the time she arrived, and Perez, the shed overseer, spotted her and came to ask after her injuries. Having assured him that she was well on the mend, Francesca looked at the freighter standing off-shore and frowned furiously. 'I understood Señor Morales to say that the boat was due later,' she said, and the man pulled a wry face, waving an extravagant hand at the large gathering of cloud over the expanse of blue sky.

'There is a storm coming, *señorita*, and it must be done quick. That is why the green boat come quicker, to miss the storm.'

'I see.' She had heard of the kind of storms these islands were subject to and the prospect of being caught in one gave her a kind of fluttering sensation in her stomach, a kind of mingled fear and excitement. 'Somebody else is running for shelter too,' she said, and pointed.

'Ah, *si señorita*; *la goleta*.'

Francesca watched the schooner coming fast before a freshening wind, ploughing wide white furrows with its bow. 'It looks beautiful,' she said, though she thought Perez failed to appreciate her admiration.

'The captain of the green boat says that there is a passenger aboard *la goleta*, *señorita*; someone from the big island.'

It took only a moment for realisation to dawn and when it did Francesca felt her heart drumming wildly in anticipation. 'You—you mean Señor Andrés is coming back?'

'*Si, señorita*.' It was difficult to tell just what Perez's reaction was to the news, but his nod confirmed it. 'The captain spoke with the captain of *la goleta* only last evening and he told him that Señor Andrés is crossing with him this morning.' He looked at the schooner racing before the gathering storm and nodded his head. 'Only a very short time now and he be in,' he observed with the surety of an expert in such matters. 'He will beat the storm easy.'

Francesca was certain Andrés had not told his grand-mother of his decision to come home, for Cecilia Morales would never have been able to keep the knowledge to herself, nor would she have had any reason to, and Francesca's first thought was to let her know. 'I must tell Señora Morales he's coming, Señor Perez! And Señor Morales too.'

'If you wish, *señorita*,' Perez told her, 'I will telephone to the *señora* and tell her. There is a connection in my office directly to *la casa*.'

'Oh, would you?' Francesca accepted the offer gladly. 'Then I can go and find Señor Morales and let him know; I know where I can find him.'

'That is what I thought, *señorita*,' Perez murmured, and Francesca caught a look of amusement in his eye that brought swift colour to her cheeks.

'There isn't a phone through to the village, is there?' she asked, and the man shook his head. 'Then I'll go and see if I can find him.'

As she made her way back along the main track the sea was out of sight, but she thanked heaven that the schooner was bound to be in at any moment now. The wind was much more brisk, and from the signs and gestures she was given as she passed, she gathered she was being warned of the approaching storm.

But there was time enough if she went by a slightly shorter route that she had discovered on the one and only other occasion she had visited the village. Even so it was a long walk and hurrying made her hot and breathless as she took the narrow track through the only uncultivated part of the island. It would be worthwile, she thought, for the satisfaction of telling Antonio that her visit to Andrés had not been in vain after all.

A cluster of neat little houses had been built in a clearing made by uprooting the trees and underbush, and were of necessity close to one another. Even so, each one had its own patch of ground growing fruit and vegetables, and pigs, goats and chickens mingled in happy proximity with the children who eyed her approach with giggling shyness and had to be coaxed into speaking with her.

From them Francesca elicited the information in Spanish that Señor Morales had gone to the tiny school, but when she enquired for him there the young school teacher shrugged. *El señor* had left some time earlier and had, she thought, been making for the groves. Almost Francesca gave up, but instead she asked the girl to tell him the news she had, in case he should return and she missed him, then she too set off towards the citrus groves. By then the fluffy white cumulus had changed to glowering grey, but she chose to disregard the ominous change.

She should perhaps have taken heed and given up, but the desire to find Antonio and tell him that his son had come home was irresistible and she went on. The clouds loomed low over the tree tops, sweeping along before the rising wind like dark-sailed galleons, and there was a kind of expectancy in the air; a brooding stillness, despite the rising wind. The intermittent growl of thunder grew in frequency and volume, but it wasn't far to the groves now and Francesca felt she had come too far to turn back.

It was unbearably hot and her shirt clung to her back in the stifling humidity, so that she opened another couple of buttons down the front of it as she made her way along the narrow track. Behind her she heard children's voices and a sudden shrill shriek of alarm at a clap of thunder, louder than the rest and almost overhead. It was followed by a peal of nervous laughter and then the call of an adult voice, shrill with warning.

Perhaps she should have gone back; Antonio would be the first to condemn her for her foolhardiness, but it seemed such a waste of effort if she did not at least make an attempt to find him. She found it harder to find her way about the groves than through the more orderly rows of bananas and she was not quite sure where she was when the rain started.

Coming on with such sudden fury that it was like being attacked by a flurry of blows.

The wind roared, bending the trees and ripping off leaves, while the rain cut like knives through the air, sharp and silver, and bruising in its hardness. Everything shivered and bowed before it, and there was nowhere she could go except along the track she was already on, because for one thing she had no idea which way to go. In the downpour it was impossible to see more than a foot in front of her, even if she had known her way through the maze of creaking trunks and lashing branches.

It was her first experience of a tropical storm and Francesca was finding it more terrifying than she would have believed possible as she went blindly on. She held her hands in front of her in a vain attempt to shield her face, for the rain pelted her relentlessly, and her thin shirt and trousers were soon soaked through and clung to her like a second skin.

Antonio would think her a complete fool, she had no doubt at all, and the worst part was that she could find little to say in her own defence. Slipping and stumbling between the trees, she acknowledged the fact that she had had no good and sensible reason for putting herself in the position she was in, soaked to the skin and sliding uncontrollably on streaming mud. She had simply wanted to tell him something he would have found out for himself soon enough anyway, and she did not anticipate or expect sympathy.

Both feet skidded from under her suddenly and she was on her knees in the mud, but as she hauled herself to her feet she spotted what looked like a thick clump of undergrowth, just off to her left, and immediately she started towards it. It appeared, as far as she could tell, to be a tangled mass of vines and shrubbery, so thick that the pelting rain scarcely penetrated it.

Hurrying as best she could, she halted suddenly and

turned, almost falling to her knees again, but sure she had heard someone calling. Her heart was thudding as she stood there, wondering if she was merely being fooled by the incredible din of the storm. But then she heard it again, and much more distinctly this time.

'Francesca!'

The voice was distorted, but the figure was unmistakable even in the unfamiliar bulk of a dark raincoat, and she stood leaning into the wind as Antonio came towards her. Whether or not he was furious with her for not heeding his warning, she neither knew nor cared at the moment; the only thing she was certain of was that she was glad to see him.

He said nothing, but grabbed her roughly and literally hauled her across to the likely cover she had already located, and which turned out to be a low, lean-to shelter of brush-wood, overgrown with vines and a mass of undergrowth. It was a rough refuge, but it was dry to some extent and Antonio pushed her down and under its sparse protection, then squashed himself in beside her.

His head was bare and he ran both hands through the thick hair falling across his forehead and dripping with rain, but in the cramped confines of the lean-to his proximity was solidly comforting. Her own red hair appeared almost as dark as his, plastered down to her head and clinging to her cheeks, and drops of moisture clung to thick lashes, then rolled down her stinging cheeks like tears.

Heaven knew who the shelter had been designed for, but it wasn't possible to sit upright in it and Francesca found it most comfortable to rest on her elbows and face outwards into the blinding rain. It was several moments before Antonio looked at her, and he was so close that every line about his mouth and eyes seemed more deeply etched into the darkly tanned face as he raised his voice above the noise of the storm.

'Why?' he demanded without preliminary, and gazed at her rain-whipped cheeks and quivering mouth sternly. 'Did I not warn you that a storm had been forecast and tell you—*suggest* that you did not go too far from shelter? Could you not see and hear it approaching?'

Francesca shifted slightly and rested her chin on folded arms as she regarded the downpour outside. 'I came to find you,' she told him, but already anticipated his opinion of her motives so that she sounded defensive and slightly reproachful. 'Perez told me that Andrés was coming on a schooner that was making for the island, and I wanted to let you know.'

'So that you could boast of how successful you had been as an advocate, I suppose!'

At the ungracious response she turned her head swiftly and glared at him. 'Nothing of the kind!' she denied. 'I just thought you'd like to know that Andrés was home again, that's all!'

'I was told when I returned to the village!'

Francesca could catch only a glimpse of his face from the corner of her eye and it was irresistible to ask, 'And you didn't want to go and see him right away?'

'Naturally I wish to see him,' Antonio agreed quietly. 'But there were other matters which seemed to me to be of more immediate importance, and Andrés will be there when I return.'

'And you never eat humble pie for anyone, do you?' she retorted promptly. 'You wouldn't go home right away, as soon as you heard, and tell him how glad you were to see him! You'd hate him to know how much you've wanted him back but were too proud and stubborn to admit it, wouldn't you?'

'Francesca! Stop before you are sorry!'

She was already sorry, Francesca realised, and when she spoke again her tone was more wistful than condemning.

'Oh, I *wish* you'd gone straight home to see him,' she said. 'What could possibly be more important than seeing your son again after all this time?'

'Finding and possibly helping someone who seems incapable of helping herself,' said Antonio. 'Andrés' absence was self-imposed, but he is a born survivor and I doubt he will ever come to much harm, young as he is—he is a Morales. But you——'

When she glanced at him briefly Francesca found herself looking into eyes that regarded her with shivering intensity. It hadn't even occurred to her that, given a choice, he would come looking for her instead of hurrying to be reunited with his son, and realising it brought a strange kind of excitement, so that she hastily averted her eyes again.

'I—I didn't realise,' she murmured, and felt that slightly unnerving gaze still on her.

'Very obviously,' he observed dryly. 'When I learned from the schoolteacher that Andrés had returned, I also learned that you had gone looking for me and I realised that you had no idea what a storm can mean in the islands. Knowing your penchant for getting into dangerous situations I thought it a wise precaution to come and find you before you came to further harm.'

Not altogether pleased with his view of her past experiences, Francesca felt bound to object. 'It's hardly been my fault that things have—happened to me since I came here——'

'Whatever the cause,' Antonio insisted, 'you seem to be prone to accident, and it was with that in mind that I came to look for you. In this instance the fault was entirely your own, for you had been warned about the approach of a storm, and whatever your motive was for going on when it must have been quite obvious the storm was about to break, it was foolish to come so far.'

Francesca kept her gaze outward, watching the unceasing

rain, and she hoped he wouldn't see how her mouth was trembling. It was an incongruous place to carry on such a conversation and in other circumstances she might even have found it amusing. But she was actually hurt by his remarks and his determined belittling of her efforts to find him, and bewildered that it should be so.

'It seemed to become so violent so quickly,' she ventured in her own defence. 'I didn't realise it would be so—so frighteningly fierce.'

'You are frightened?'

Obviously it had not even occurred to him, and Francesca wondered what effect it would have if she professed to being frightened. 'Not so much frightened as—as stunned,' she confessed. 'I've never seen anything like this before, and I was soaked to the skin in seconds.'

'But of course, in such thin clothing!' he said, and Francesca turned a reproachful shoulder to him.

'You're so sympathetic and understanding!'

Being so tall Antonio could not stretch out full length as she did, but half sat, half crouched under the low top of the shelter. He had raised himself as far from the ground as he was able and Francesca realised that he was unfastening the bulky raincoat he wore, no easy task in such cramped conditions.

'I don't want your raincoat,' she told him hastily. 'It isn't worth it, I'm already soaked.'

Antonio eased his right arm from the sleeve and looked at her with a certain glint in her eyes that was infinitely disturbing. 'I was not proposing to give it to you,' he informed her, 'merely to share it.' Lifting his right arm, he stretched the raincoat wide. 'Come!' he urged quietly. 'Move up closer.'

Francesca was shivering, she realised, though she was certain that it had nothing to do with being chilled because her whole body seemed to be on fire, and the colour burned in her cheeks as she hesitated to do as he said. Then she obediently inched along the ground until she was close against the warm vibrance of him, and shivered again when the arm descended like a dark wing across her shoulders, half smothering her in the bulky raincoat. His fingers curved into her upper arm and she was pressed hard to his long length with every nerve in her body responding to the touch of him.

'O.K.?' he enquired, and she nodded.

With his free hand he reached across and stroked the strands of wet hair from her face, his long fingers gentle, almost sensuous in their touch and alarmingly affecting. The rain continued to hiss its fury, and every so often a little flurry of it splashed their faces, but for the most part they were high and dry. The tiny shelter was simple and crude, but it was built on a bank higher than the surrounding ground and the water drained away from it, the prevailing wind blowing in from behind its sloping roof. To Francesca there was more danger in the proximity of the man beside her than in the storm, and even in the silence between them there was a kind of tingling anticipation.

'How—how long will it last?'

Her voice sounded small and shiveringly unsteady, and she dared not turn her head for fear of finding her face too near to his; that firm, passionate mouth attracted her too strongly to risk it coming closer. Apparently Antonio had no such hesitation, for when he replied to her query his breath fluttered warmly against her cheek.

'Not for very much longer now, I think.' His long fingers curved more deeply into her arm for a moment. 'Are you too uncomfortable?'

'Oh no, I'm fine!'

Every breath he took brought a renewed awareness of the fierce virility of him, and the pressure of his arm across her shoulders made it impossible for her to move even slightly away from him. In her heart Francesca admitted to not wanting to move away, but the thought was dangerous, she told herself, and Antonio Morales was not some pleasantly ordinary boy-friend whom she could manage quite easily if he tried to take advantage of their situation.

Fortunately she was able to keep her gaze forward, watching the almost solid sheet of rain that ripped through the grove like an army of scythes, but it was harder to control the response of her body, and her breathing had become deeper and more exaggerated, so that she tried to make conversation to cover the fact.

'Does—does it do a lot of damage? I mean, will there be a lot of the fruit damaged? Even at home, where we don't have anything remotely like this, there's very often a lot of damage, and this seems as if it's actually tearing the leaves from the trees.'

'It is not quite so bad as it was, I think.' Antonio's quiet response served to remind her of how garrulous she sounded and she realised there was a slight lessening of the fury outside their shelter. Until that moment Francesca had kept her head averted by sheer willpower, but she sensed the slow gaze that moved over her features as if committing them to memory. Her skin prickled as if cool fingers smoothed over it caressingly, and it was irresistible when she eventually did turn her head. '*Does* it frighten you, Francesca?'

'Oh no, not—not frighten me.'

'*Bueno*,' he approved softly, and it was suddenly impossible not to keep looking up at him.

His skin glowed like burnished bronze with the rain, and the thick lashes surrounding his blue eyes were spikily wet, like the swathe of hair across his forehead. It was an unconscious movement when she half turned to face him, and the clinging wet shirt parted lower still when it was caught under her, revealing the soft curving swell of her bosom in a deep plunge of pale cream lawn.

His eyes seemed darker, shadowed by heavy lids, and gleaming with a warmth she had seen there only once before. He was already so close that it took no more than a slight shifting of his weight to press hard against her trembling body, and she lifted her arms intuitively, her hands seeking to bring his head down to her.

His mouth touched hers, light and gentle for a moment, then suddenly almost savage in its demand, and Francesca responded because there was nothing else she could do. She seemed almost to have stopped breathing, and a whole new gamut of sensations roused and teased her mind and body until she forgot even where she was.

Long hands, unexpectedly trembling, slid the shirt down from her shoulders and he buried his face in the warm curve between neck and shoulders, his mouth pressed hungrily to soft, damp skin. From the pulsing warmth of her throat and neck down to the cleft of shadow between her breasts; deep, fervent kisses that fed her own unfamiliar passion.

As she soared to unbelievable heights Francesca pressed persuasive fingers into a lean back, sensitive tips touching every muscle that rippled below warm flesh, only thinly disguised by a slightly damp shirt. But for all her readiness to yield, for all the wild, almost uncontrollable need she felt, alarm was mingled with excitement and desire suddenly when the bruisingly hard weight of his body bore down on her fiercely.

She was forced on to her back, the stony ground agonisingly painful and bringing from her a small whimper of protest as she turned her head from side to side in a daze of emotion. Immediately Antonio raised his head and looked down at her with a burning brightness in his eyes that tempered slowly to realisation.

'Francesca!' His voice was harsh and he wrapped both arms tightly around her, holding her against him, with one hand cradling her head to the heaving warmth of his chest and his face resting on her wet hair. 'Oh, little one, I go too far—too quickly! I forget that you are so——' His lips were pressed for a moment to her forehead. '*Nena! Lo siento mucho*, Francesca, I think only of my own desires!'

Again she felt the brush of his lips on her forehead and she kept her eyes closed, revelling in the hard virility of him even while her brain tingled a warning. She murmured something, even she did not know what she said, and he again kissed her, still speaking in that mixture of English and Spanish, and holding her breathtakingly close.

It was not like Antonio to be sorry for anything he did, and yet he seemed genuinely anxious to impress upon her how sorry he was, so that it eventually dawned on her that he was apologising so profusely because he thought he had alarmed her with the heat of his passion. On more than one occasion he had remarked on the fact that she was not so very much older than his son, and she suspected it was that which now made him apologise so earnestly. What surprised her was just how much she disliked being reminded of it.

'I am forgiven?'

The words fluttered against the nape of her neck as she rested her face on his chest, and she nodded as best she could for the hand that curved its long fingers about her head. She wanted to tell him that she was not an ingenuous child, but a grown woman, old enough to be vitally aware of him as a man. But for the moment she said nothing.

It was quiet, she realised suddenly, as if the storm had subsided with that dangerous mood of abandon. The wind had dropped and the rain was no more than a last shower, silvered by the sun reappearing in a rapidly lightening sky. The touch of Antonio's shirt against her bare skin reminded her of how vulnerably naked she was, and she stirred briefly, reaching with one hand to try and close the gaping front of her shirt.

But the movement, slight as it was, broke the spell and Antonio eased her away from him, looking deep into her eyes from only inches away. A look of gentle concern that confirmed Francesca's suspicion that he regarded her as too young and too defenceless for someone of his maturity and experience.

'You must not become chilled,' he said softly, and resting on one elbow he pulled her shirt up around her shoulders. Lightly and deftly he covered her nakedness, and the touch of his long brown fingers was shiveringly evocative as he fastened all but the top two buttons of her shirt. 'So!'

He turned and peered out from the shelter, and Francesca found it hard to believe that he was actually avoiding her eyes. 'It—it seems to have stopped,' she ventured, and her voice was small and unsteady only because she could still imagine the touch of his hands.

'*Sì*,' he agreed quietly. 'Shall we go?'

When she nodded, he smiled briefly, then turned and crawled out into the open, stretching his long length in relief before bending to offer her his hands. The rain was not completely stopped, but Francesca thought it was little use offering that as an excuse to stay for a while longer. So she took the proffered hands, allowing herself to be pulled up to her feet, but feeling oddly vulnerable when she stood beside him.

'O.K.?' Antonio asked, keeping hold of her hands for a moment, and she nodded. 'You see,' he went on with an extravagant sweep of one hand. 'Did I not tell you that it would not last for very long?'

It seemed to Francesca that his mood of lightness was almost forced, and her own feelings were still confused. He seemed to be reassuring her as he would a child, when only moments ago she had surely proved herself a woman. Only that fateful and involuntary whimper had snatched them both back from complete abandonment, and she wished she was more sure whether or not she regretted it.

Her silence and the air about her drew his attention, and he was looking down at her with a slight frown, studying her face closely. The slight thrust of her lower lip was unmistakable and she did not even thank him for helping her to her feet, but kept her eyes downcast and her gaze on the top button of his shirt.

'Francesca?' A long finger slid beneath her chin and lifted it, showing him her expression more clearly. 'Have I angered you so much?' he asked softly, and Francesca wished she did not find his gentleness so disarming.

'You haven't angered me at all!' she denied swiftly, but quite clearly it was an untruth and Antonio still frowned.

'That is obviously not true, Francesca.'

'Good heavens,' she declared in desperation, 'I've been kissed before, why should I be angry?'

'So you have told me,' said Antonio, and the more familiar edge was on his voice, she noticed. 'But if you are not angry, why are you looking as you do? Your lip pouted, and your eyes unwilling to look at me! I am sorry for what I did, Francesca, and I promise that I will never let it happen again, but I am——'

'That's what you said before!' Francesca interrupted petulantly, 'But you never seem to be able to decide whether to treat me like a woman or a five-year-old child, and I wish you'd make up your mind!'

He was silent for several seconds, then she caught a glimpse of the deep dark look in his eyes as he turned away from her. 'When *you* decide which you are, *niña*, then I will make up my mind! Now you will return to the house with me and get out of those wet clothes as soon as possible! Come!'

'Are you on foot?'

The question had only just occurred to her, and Francesca looked at him curiously. She had heard nothing of a horse when he came to find her and yet it wasn't like him to be on foot. Antonio stopped and half turned, watching her with a curious expression in the depth of his eyes. 'The mare was alarmed by the storm and so I left her in the *aldea*. If you walk back that far then you can ride behind me back to the house.'

It was a tempting offer, but having just about recovered from the effect of such close proximity, Francesca shied away from repeating the experience so soon. 'I'd rather walk, thank you,' she told him, but knew she was going to meet opposition even before she had finished speaking.

'Walk with me as far as the *aldea* and I will send Jose for you,' he said, and again she was tempted. When she shook her head, then Antonio exploded into anger. 'You have the impudence to call me stubborn, and yet you refuse to take the quickest and most comfortable way, even though you are soaked to your skin! *Madre mia*, Francesca, I shall soon lose my temper with you if you do not behave!'

Francesca glared at him indignantly and would have objected, but he reached for her left hand and almost crushed her fingers with the hard strong pressure of his. Then giving her a slight shake as he drew her alongside him, he started for the village, giving her little option but to go too, and making very little allowance for her shorter stride as she squelched along in her wet shoes.

'You will wait under cover until I send Jose with the *carruaje*,' he told her firmly, 'and you will ride back, *niña*, however much fuss you make!'

'You're a bully!'

'I am out of patience!' Antonio retorted.

However much she berated him, Francesca made no attempt to free the hand he held so tightly, and as she walked in apparent submission at his side, she remembered the raincoat he had been wearing when he came to look for her. It was still raining, and she wondered what reason he would give for having left it in the rough little shelter they had shared—providing anyone ever had the temerity to question him, of course.

CHAPTER SEVEN

IT was Cecilia Morales who, not unexpectedly, decided that there should be a very special dinner that evening to celebrate her grandson's homecoming, and Francesca quite happily went along with the idea. She doubted if she had made things any easier for herself in the future by persuading Andrés to come back to Trader's Cay, but his grandmother was happier than she had been for weeks, and Francesca knew that in his heart Antonio was too.

Because the evening was going to be something more than their usual informal meal, Francesca took the opportunity to dress up a little, and put on her prettiest dress. Normally she needed only an ordinary day dress for dinner and there had never been occasion to bring out one of the few evening dresses she possessed. With the chance to make the most of herself for once, she took extra care with every detail and revelled in the opportunity.

It was not until she was taking a really close look at herself in the bedroom mirror that she realised there was something very different about her reflection. The difference was not easy to define exactly, but it was there, and she turned away from the image of herself feeling strangely disturbed. But even the act of turning around seemed to emphasise differences that she was reluctant to recognise.

She found it all too easy to recall the possessive strength

of Antonio's arms, the urgent demanding pressure of his mouth, and the fierce virility to which she had so nearly succumbed. It was an experience that would stay with her for the rest of her life, she felt convinced, and something of the passion he had kindled still lingered in her eyes and in the movement of her body. It was from the reflected image of a more sexually aware woman that she turned so hastily, because she found it too disturbing.

Just briefly she glanced once more in the mirror before she turned to go, and realised she had chosen that particular dress tonight because it suited the new image of herself. Antonio could not fail to appreciate the effect of its deep coppery-gold colour with her own colouring, nor the bodice that was loosely draped with cunning softness over the rounded curves of her bosom, showing glimpses of pale skin that were far more provocative than nakedness. And the skirt that swirled in loose folds, concealing but at the same time suggesting the slender shape beneath.

Francesca had never felt more aware of her own body than she did as she came slowly down the wide staircase, her long skirt lifted in one hand and her heart beating fast. She knew she looked good, better than ever before, and yet she felt a curious sensation of anxiety too, because she could not anticipate Antonio's reaction to the glowing warmth of her mood. He was certainly experienced enough to put his own construction on her new awareness, but how would he react to it?

He had said scarcely a word to her since he left her in one of the village houses to await Jose with the carriage, with the threat of dire consequences if she did not do as he said. He had been rather involved with Andrés, it was true, but still she had the feeling that he might almost have gone out of his way to avoid speaking to her, and it was a situation she had to admit she didn't like.

She put a hand to her copper red hair, bouncy and shiningly clean after its soaking earlier in the day, and a wonderful contrast to the creamy skin that redheads are so often endowed with. Her green eyes glowing between thick brown lashes, bathed and perfumed, she looked very different from the bedraggled mudlark who had arrived home soaking wet and obediently riding in Señora Morales' carriage. There was nothing that could mar her enjoying this evening, she vowed.

As she came down into the hall someone opened the door of Antonio's study, and she immediately turned her head, her heartbeat suddenly so violent that it literally took her breath away. But disappointment came almost at once when she saw that it was Andrés and not Antonio who came across the hall on his way to the *salón*, and the reaction showed briefly in her eyes.

'*Buenas tardes*, Señorita Dale.' Andrés greeted her very formally in Spanish. But he paused in his stride when he was opposite the foot of the stairs and the way he glanced quickly over her from head to foot was reminiscent of the way his father always scrutinised her. Only Andrés' survey lacked Antonio's warmth of appraisal, and she felt no response from her senses in this instance.

Obviously Andrés too had complied with his grandmother's decision to make the evening one of formal celebration, for he was wearing evening dress, slim-fitting trousers and a well-tailored white dinner jacket that in the first few moments when she recognised him made him look slightly older. Of impeccable cut, it disguised some of his boyish thinness and emphasised his darkly handsome looks; and he was stunningly handsome, she had to admit.

Nevertheless Francesca approached him warily, for she was not quite sure what to expect. For one thing she did not quite understand why he should be waiting for her to join him, for it was not the kind of thing that she would have expected of him, and she scarcely believed it when he smiled. In an effort to throw off her lingering suspicion of him she fluffed out the skirt of her long dress and smiled too.

'All in your honour, Andrés,' she told him, and he inclined his head gravely.

'I am honoured, *señorita*.'

Impulsive as always, Francesca sought to bridge the barrier between them, although she still half expected to be snubbed for her trouble, and was aware of sounding slightly breathless. 'I wish you'd call me Francesca, Andrés. Señora Morales and your father do—won't you?'

'If it is what you wish.'

Not a very encouraging start, Francesca thought, and found herself wishing Antonio was there to lend her his support. 'It would be more friendly,' she suggested. 'Don't you think?'

Andrés again inclined his head in apparent agreement and walked beside her, stepping ahead to open the *salón* door for her. Just for a moment when she walked past him into the room he caught her eye, held it, then lowered his gaze again. 'Francesca,' he murmured, and it was almost possible to believe she heard his father's voice, except that there was the rawness of youth in the deep timbre of it.

The *salón* was empty and again Francesca felt that curious sense of anxiety at the thought of being alone with Andrés. She could never bring herself to trust this tall and incredibly handsome son of Antonio's, and he made her feel far more uncomfortable than his father did. Antonio was arrogant and implacable and she knew the fury he could be roused to, but she had experienced first hand just how callously cruel Andrés could be; something that Antonio, whatever his faults, never was.

She accepted his offer of a drink and he handed her a glass of sherry with solemn politeness, raising his own glass in a toast. '*Salud!*'

In the silence that followed Francesca got the feeling that he had something on his mind. He looked vaguely troubled, as if he was not quite sure how to express what it was that troubled him, and it served to remind her that, in years, he was little more than a schoolboy. Thinking to distract him from whatever it was, she smiled.

'I'm really glad that you decided to come home, Andrés.'

He looked at her for a moment and Francesca glimpsed something of the more familiar mockery in his eyes, then he took another sip from his glass and concealed their expression with lowered lids. 'I cannot believe you are, Francesca,' he said.

'But I am, honestly!'

He smiled faintly, still giving his attention to the clear amber liquid in his glass. 'I can believe that you are thankful for Abuela's sake, and perhaps for my father's, for I know he welcomes me, but I find it difficult to accept that you welcome me back when I have been so—unfriendly towards you in the past.'

As an understatement that took some beating when she considered his almost murderous behaviour, and Francesca smiled ruefully to herself. The sentiments he expressed were more likely to be his grandmother's than his own, she thought, and Antonio would definitely have worded it much more strongly. 'You certainly made it pretty clear that you didn't want me here,' she said, choosing her words with care, 'but I suppose in the circumstances you felt you had the right to resent me coming.'

'My father also,' Andrés insisted, and Francesca acknowledged it with a grimace.

'Only his methods were much more subtle,' she told him. Remembering her indignation that first morning, when she had been knocked up at six-thirty and expected to ride a horse when she had never been on one in her life before, made her smile now, but it had not been funny at the time.

'Even so, they didn't work either,' she added. 'I quite enjoyed the routine when I got used to it.'

'You still ride?'

Francesca nodded, remembering too another attempt by Antonio to keep her in line. 'I intend to as soon as my arm's strong enough,' she said. 'I'm not ready to give up Trader's Cay to please either of you, Andrés, but I would like there to be more—understanding between us. I'm prepared to overlook what's happened in the past and start again from the beginning, if you are.'

'*Gracias*, Francesca!'

There was possibly a hint of sarcasm in his reply, but Francesca had meant it when she said she wanted to begin again, so she did not take him up. It was the only way she could go on living at Trader's Cay, and her resolve was no nearer weakening than it had been that first day. Although possibly if she gave herself time to consider, her reasons for wanting to stay were rather different now.

Andrés drained his glass and stood twirling the slender stem between his fingers while Francesca eyed him curiously. She did not expect a complete about-face where her position was concerned, for such dramatic changes of heart do not happen in real life. And yet this formally polite and serious young man bore little resemblance to the bold and arrogant tormentor of her early days at Trader's Cay, and she could only suppose that he still had something on his mind.

'You're very solemn,' she told him, attempting to keep it light and casual. 'Have you got something on your mind, Andrés?'

When he turned and put down his glass, Francesca noticed how he glanced over his shoulder at the door, as if he feared they might be interrupted. Her pulse fluttered for a moment when she noticed it, for she wasn't really sure if she wanted to be taken into his confidence if it was something that was likely to antagonise Antonio.

Andrés did not look at her, but traced the pattern on the edge of the ornately carved sideboard with a fingertip. 'It is not polite to burden others with one's problems,' he said, and Francesca eyed him doubtfully.

Lack of politeness had never bothered him in the past and she was tempted to remind him of it, but somehow his manner suggested he was very much preoccupied with whatever it was he had on his mind. He was young and maybe he needed someone to confide in other than his father or his grandmother, and she genuinely did want to come to a better understanding with him if it was possible. For Antonio's sake as much as her own, she realised, and smiled a little uncertainly at his son.

'If it will help to talk about—whatever it is, please do,' she told him. 'Although I can't help thinking that your grandmother would almost certainly be a better person to confide in.'

'Not in this instance,' Andrés denied, and turned his head again, instantly alert. Someone was coming across the hall and the firm tread was unmistakably Antonio's. Andrés obviously recognised it too, for he shook his head and raised both hands in a gesture of resignation. 'It is not possible now,' he said, speaking swiftly and lowering his voice. 'If you will meet me after *cena*. In the garden, perhaps.'

A little startled at the idea of a secret meeting in the garden, Francesca just managed to nod automatic consent before the door opened and Antonio came in. She felt she looked guilty, and his quick glance from one to the other seemed to confirm it, but then he gave a barely perceptible shrug and checked that she had a drink before helping himself.

Francesca tried not to stare, but she found it impossible not to. In anything he wore Antonio was a staggeringly attractive man, but in a well-cut dinner jacket and groomed to perfection he presented another facet altogether. There was about him an almost regal air, an emphasis on the arrogance that she now admitted was an integral part of his attraction, and he conveyed all the authority and sublime pride of generations of Morales as he stood there with his back half turned to her while he poured himself a drink.

Her emotions reacted more wildly than they ever had before, and she was unaware of anything but the fact that it filled her with an unbelievable sense of elation to remember how she had been in his arms that morning, and felt the fierce ardour of his mouth on hers. When he turned from the sideboard, glass in hand, he caught her look and smiled faintly before she quickly glanced away.

'*Salud!*' he said, and somehow managed to give it a quite different meaning from what Andrés did.

By now, Francesca thought, she should have been accustomed to that long slow survey that took note of every detail of her person and her dress, but on this occasion its scrutiny seemed so much more explicit. It reminded her of the intimacy of a small brushwood shelter and of the tempting proximity of a lean virile body, and she felt the colour flood into her face.

'There are obviously advantages to dressing for dinner,' he remarked, and raised his glass again in a silent salute. 'That color suits you very well, Francesca, and a dress is so much more feminine than a shirt, in most circumstances.'

Without the memory of that morning to sense hidden meaning in the words, the compliment would have seemed ordinary enough, but she recalled how clinging and feminine a wet shirt could be, and had no doubt that Antonio remembered too. Andrés, she could sense, was puzzled by her reaction, and it must surely have lent strength to Antonio's suspicion that she was young and inexperienced, when she blushed like a schoolgirl at a simple compliment.

'It isn't often I get the chance to dress up,' she said, holding tight to her wavering composure. 'This is the first time since I came here.'

'Perhaps we should do it more often,' Antonio suggested. 'Although I admit that for myself, I prefer something a little less formal.'

'Oh, but you look so——' Francesca could have bitten out her tongue, but it was too late to do anything about it now. That impulsive response could have left him in little doubt of her opinion, and she went on hurriedly in an attempt to cover her embarrassment. 'I think we all look so much more elegant in evening dress, don't you? I've never worn this dress before and it feels——' She lifted her shoulders slightly and the silky material slid with sensual softness over her skin, like caressing fingers. 'Besides,' she added quickly when she recalled long brown hands making the same sensual caress, 'it's good for my morale!'

'Oh, but surely your morale is in no such need, is it, Francesca?' Antonio suggested quietly, and regarded her above the rim of his glass as he said it.

'A figure of speech, that's all,' she insisted, and noticed he smiled faintly.

But he no longer looked at her when he went on. 'You perhaps miss your own friends. I imagine that you were very much in demand for parties and dates; the English male is not, I believe, as—backward as is sometimes supposed.'

It was hard not to attribute more than the casual interest his tone suggested, and Francesca wondered if he saw her earlier life at home as one round of pleasure with endless boy-friends. 'I had dates,' she said, watching his expression from the thickness of her lashes. 'I worked in an office in town and it's almost impossible to stay at home when you know a lot of people, even if you *did* want to. I liked going out; not to parties so much, but to restaurants and theatres.'

'Which you surely miss, living here?' he suggested, and glanced at Andrés. 'I know that Andrés missed those things when he returned from school in Madrid.'

A glance at Andrés' sober face and downcast eyes suggested that he still missed the city life; much as his mother had, she remembered. 'A lot depends on your outlook,' Francesca stated carefully, unwilling to become involved in a discussion that included Andrés' feelings. 'Personally I rather enjoy the life here. I must admit that at first I missed certain things, but now——' She studiously avoided looking at him, and instead gazed into the liquid in her glass. 'Now I'd like to spend the rest of my life here.'

Antonio was watching her, she knew it, she could feel the intensity of his gaze without even looking at him, and she wondered if he had any inkling of why she had made that rash claim about wanting to stay at Trader's Cay for the rest of her life. Andrés too, she realised, had been waiting to hear her reply, though not with quite the same intensity as his father had.

'Is there no one you wish to return to?' Antonio asked, in the deeply soft voice that could so easily be her undoing in certain circumstances, and she shook her head.

'No one important enough to influence me. I shouldn't have been so ready to come out to the Caribbean if there had been.'

'You would not have been prepared to sacrifice a lover in favour of becoming part-owner of Tradaro's?' he insisted, and again she shook her head.

'No, of course not!' She was quite adamant, and yet Francesca was certain that only if the hypothetical lover had been a man after his like would she have been prepared to sacrifice her claim to Trader's Cay for him.

'Would you really have given up your claim for a man you loved?'

Francesca turned swiftly, reminded suddenly of Andrés' presence, and nodded her head insistently. 'If I'd really loved someone nothing in the world would have induced me to leave him.'

She could be adamant because she thought she had some idea of what it would be like in a situation like that, and the man who made her so certain was the same one who apparently took such an interest in her reaction. She recognised how close she was to falling in love with Antonio, and somehow the thought dismayed her. In part because she felt very sure that any woman in his life must inevitably play a subordinate role to Trader's Cay, just as Ana Morales had. She must therefore do her best not to let it happen.

'Anyway, as there isn't anyone, the question doesn't arise, does it?' she said, and hastily drank the last drop of her sherry as Cecilia Morales came in to join them, breathing a sigh of relief at her timing.

Conversation during dinner was mostly concerned with what Andrés had been doing during his absence, although Francesca felt certain that at least some of the episodes he related with great attention to detail for the amusement of his grandmother, were greatly exaggerated if not sheer fiction. Antonio occasionally made a contribution which suggested that he was inclined to share Francesca's view, but Señora Morales was content that her beloved Andrés was home again and she was an appreciative audience.

'And now you will stay with us, eh, *muchacho*?' she beamed, obviously taking it for granted that no such crisis would arise again. 'No more will you make your *abuela* unhappy by leaving her, eh?'

It was fortunate that his grandmother had such faith in her own forecast and she missed the fact that instead of confirming it, Andrés glanced across at Francesca with a curious expression in his eyes that she failed to interpret. If Antonio had noticed he gave no sign, but raised the matter of the damage done by that morning's storm.

'Your assistance has been missed,' he told him. 'I shall be thankful to have you back again.' In that instance he did notice the oddly evasive shrug of Andrés' shoulders, however, and disregarding his coffee for a moment he frowned at his son curiously. 'You do intend to go to work with me again?' he asked, and again Andrés shrugged in a way that offered neither confirmation nor denial, and for a moment Antonio regarded him with narrowed eyes. 'Ah, but of course you will,' he said, seemingly confident. 'What else would you do but safeguard the continued prosperity of your inheritance?'

'Mine and Francesca's,' Andrés reminded him with a hint of malice, and Antonio frowned as if he had actually forgotten the fact.

'Of course,' he conceded after a second or two, and again gave his attention to coffee and brandy.

'Be in no doubt, *mi padre*,' Andrés told him, soft-voiced. 'Did you not hear Francesca say that she will stay here for the remainder of her life?' When he looked as he did at that moment Francesca had little doubt that nothing had changed where Andrés was concerned, and she felt a small flutter of fear in her stomach as she instinctively looked at Antonio. 'Of course,' Andrés began in that same soft voice, 'if anything happened, and Francesca was to——'

'If anything happens to Francesca, you shall answer to me for it!' said Antonio, and something in his voice made his mother shake her head urgently.

He added something at length, and in Spanish, and there was a gleaming brightness in his blue eyes that sent shivers through Francesca's whole being as she watched him. No one was making any pretence of drinking at the moment, and Cecilia Morales looked as if she had received a shock, her anxious eyes watching the dark, passionate face of her son, then darting with equal anxiety to the brightly flushed features of her grandson.

Francesca could have wept to see the uneasy peace that had existed before dinner shattered by a vague unspoken threat, and she reached out instinctively and placed a hand

on Antonio's arm, bringing that burning blue gaze round
to her. 'Please,' she murmured, flicking a moistening tongue
across dry lips. 'Please don't, Tonio, I——'

'Have you not yet learnt, *niña*,' Antonio interrupted
harshly, 'not to interfere in matters that do not concern
you?'

'But it *does*—it *did* concern me!' she insisted, and pressed
her fingers into the muscular resistance of his forearm.
'Please, Tonio, if——'

'If you are to remain here for the rest of your life,'
Antonio said in a voice that shook with a passion she only
half understood, 'it may be that *I* shall have to sell *my* share
and leave you undisputed owner, for you seem incapable of
allowing me to take care of my own affairs!'

'Tonio!'

Cecilia Morales sounded shocked, although it was doubt-
ful if she took the threat at face value, while Andrés did not
even look up, only sat with a faintly sinister smile on his
mouth, stirring the coffee in his cup round and round as if
mesmerised by it. It was Francesca who took it most to
heart, and she looked at him with bright gleaming green
eyes that showed both resentment and hurt.

'You wouldn't even consider selling me your share!' she
told him, confident she spoke the truth. 'You know you
wouldn't, Tonio, you attach too much importance to your
precious Tradaro's; I know you! You wouldn't part with
what you consider your birthright for any reason at all!'

Anger gave a touch of cruelty to his strong firm mouth,
but far from shrinking from it, Francesca found it curiously
exciting to be crossing swords with him again. He could
hurt her more easily than any man had ever done in her life,
and yet she could never find it in her heart to hate him for it,
nor even blame him. There was a glorious fire in his anger,
as there was in his lovemaking, that swept through her emotions and aroused a responsive passion in her.

Eyes gleaming darkly, he considered her with unwavering steadiness. 'You presume to know me well,' he observed in a deeply quiet voice, and Francesca shook her head instinctively.

'Not that,' she denied breathlessly. 'But you've never left me in any doubt about how much Trader's Cay means to you, and I can't see you giving it up simply to be rid of what you see as my interference! No woman has yet succeeded in turning you from the love of your life, and I'm not fool enough to believe *I* could!'

'Then do not be fool enough to interfere in matters that do not concern you!' Antonio returned shortly.

Maybe the ghost of Ana Morales had risen briefly in his mind too, but Francesca found herself trembling, and her emotions threatened to swamp common sense, so that getting to her feet was an almost automatic reaction. In silence she walked across the room, and it was Señora Morales' voice that showed her the impression she had given. Appalled by her son's harshness, she called after her anxiously.

'Francesca, my dear child!' Francesca opened the door, and she went on speaking urgently to her son in Spanish. 'Tonio, *váya pronto!*'

Half turned in the doorway, Francesca saw Antonio already out of his seat, and shook her head quickly. 'No! Don't come after me—please!'

Closing the door quickly, she hurried across the hall to the outside door, conscious of the murmur of Spanish in the *salón* behind her. Slipping quickly outside into the cool of the garden, she took stock of her dramatic exit and grimaced ruefully. She had no need to have reacted as she did, for almost certainly Antonio had spoken as he had only in anger, but she had reacted impulsively as she so often did.

More satisfactory was to remember the fact that he had been so swift and furious in warning his son about her future safety, for she believed he had meant that quite seriously. In fact she recognised now that both his warning to Andrés and his harsh reprimand of her were so typical of him that neither of them should have affected her the way they had.

Now that it was apparent Antonio had taken her at her word, she slowed her pace to a mere stroll and wandered on through the garden in a pensive mood. The Spanish temperament was fiery and she was beginning to grow accustomed to it, but it did not make for peaceful co-existence when her own redheaded temper had as low a flash-point. By now, she guessed, Antonio too would have recovered his own temper, but she was in no mind to go back and face them all again.

She took the path that skirted round overgrown shrubs and flowering trees and eventually led to the stable, and the profusion of scents in the night air was balm to even the most heated temper. The rain that morning had done damage, but it had also freshened the earth and the lush growth of leaves and blossoms, and she breathed it all in as she strolled along the overgrown path.

There was a curious unreality about it all in the haze of moonlight. Dark leaves gleamed like polished black leather and waxy pale blossoms peered like white faces through the foliage; hibiscus changed from rich blue to almost black and the crimson heads of oleander were darker still. A light wind whispered through the tops of immortelle and palm, and Francesca lifted her face to catch its coolness, half closing her eyes to appreciate it more.

A second later she opened them wide and turned quickly, her senses instantly alert to footsteps padding firmly along the same path she had taken. It did not even occur to her that it would be anyone other than Antonio, and she stood unmoving, but with her heart beating wildly and bringing colour to her cheeks as she watched the huge hibiscus at the bend in the path, waiting for him to appear. It became almost unbearable as the firm confident steps came nearer, and she moistened her lips with the tip of her tongue when the sleeve of a white dinner jacket came into view.

'Tonio?'

Her voice had a soft huskiness that must surely have betrayed how anxious she was for it to be him, and it was impossible to conceal her disappointment when Andrés appeared instead. Boldly handsome in the moonlight, his eyes burned like jet between their thick lashes, and there was a slightly cynical smile on his lips. It was a look that took away his youth and gave him instead the appearance of a satyr, so that she felt a sudden flick of fear at the sight of him.

It was ridiculous to fear an eighteen-year-old youth, but there was that indefinable something about Andrés that her too responsive senses reacted to. As they did to his father, in a very different way. He was smiling, a gleam of white teeth in the dark oval of his face, with a corresponding glow in his eyes suggesting amusement.

'I am sorry to disappoint you, Francesca,' he said in a soft voice. 'But you agreed to meet me here after we had eaten, if you remember.'

'Oh yes. Yes, of course, I'd forgotten.'

It was so obviously true that she saw no point in not admitting it, and Andrés regarded her for a moment with both hands thrust into the pockets of his jacket. The moonlight scattered light shadows over her face, making it hard to define any particular expression, and he seemed to be seeking some betrayal of how she felt. 'You *are* disappointed, are you not, Francesca?' he insisted. 'You would much rather it was my father who had followed you here?'

Francesca was much less willing to be frank in this instance, and she looked down at the dancing shadows at her feet rather than face that smiling and faintly mocking expression. 'When I left he looked as if he meant to come after me,' she reminded him, and Andrés nodded, still smiling.

'But you forbade him to, Francesca!'

Forbade was putting it much too strongly, and she had certainly not anticipated that Antonio would take her wishes into account if he had wanted to follow her. She turned and took a white blossom in her hand, cupping the waxen petals in her palm and gazing down at them unseeingly, and her shoulders lifted very slightly in a suggestion of a shrug. 'Your father isn't in the habit of doing as I say,' she told him. 'It wouldn't have surprised me in the least if he'd come anyway, whatever I said about it.'

She was aware that Andrés watched her still, watching for every change of expression that flitted across her face. 'And yet I believe you wanted him to come,' he insisted, and his sudden faint chuckle startled her so that she spun round to face him again, her eyes wide and plainly wary. 'You are—different,' Andrés went on, obviously confident of his facts. 'I noticed it the moment I saw you come back to the house this morning, and it set me wondering the reason for it.'

'Different?' Francesca remembered the disturbing stranger she had noticed in her bedroom mirror just before she went down to dinner, and knew exactly what he meant, though she would not dream of admitting it.

Andrés nodded, and his gleaming dark eyes never left her face while he explained his meaning, using his long expressive hands to add conviction to what he said. 'I could see it quite clearly when you returned this morning, wet and uncomfortable. You did not appear to notice the discomfort, nor did you look angry or distressed about the condition you were in.'

'You're very observant!' Her retort was swift and defensive, and there was an air of breathlessness about it that he could not fail to notice.

'You did not look as a woman does who has been drenched to her skin in a storm and hates not only the discomfort of it, but also the fact that she is not looking her best,' Andrés insisted knowledgeably. 'And this evening when you came downstairs you looked—different.'

'Andrés, you——'

'There is a look about you, Francesca,' he went on relentlessly, 'that suggests to me that my father has perhaps moved in the direction I suggested he might.'

'You're talking nonsense!'

'Am I?'

Francesca sought desperately to subdue the memory of being in Antonio's arms and the violent abandonment of those few minutes in the citrus grove while they sheltered from the storm. 'You—you're being quite ridiculous,' she accused huskily, and Andrés laughed.

'So?' he asked softly. 'He came most gallantly to your defence just a few moments ago, and there is about you the look of a woman who has been——' The gesture he made was so unmistakably explicit that Francesca jerked her head in swift denial, while the thud of her heartbeat pounded like drums through her body.

'Andrés——'

'How willingly did you succumb to persuasion, Francesca?' he taunted. 'How much persuasion would it take for you to marry him and give him complete control of Tradaro's as I suggested, eh? My father can be very persuasive with women, so I believe—when it is to his advantage, of course!'

'Stop it, Andrés!' Her face flaming, Francesca thanked heaven for the disguising moonlight while she looked up at him with bright angry eyes. 'You implied that you had something of a personal nature to talk to me about, but not my—my relationship with your father. If all you want to do is make these—these ridiculous remarks, I refuse to listen to any more! You can go away and leave me alone; I won't stand here and listen——'

'*No, no, no! Lo siento!*' Quite clearly she had shaken him with her outburst, and it was brought home to her yet again how young he was in fact. He took his hands out of his pockets and for a second or two gave his attention to smoothing down the immaculate dinner jacket while he presumably made up his mind what to say next. 'If you were interested in my father,' he began, and held up a soothing hand when she would have protested, 'it could have made some difference to what I have to say,' he insisted. 'For that reason only, I mention it again.'

Francesca wished she could trust him as she did Antonio, but her senses still shied away from the unspoken threat that always seemed to linger in those deep, dark eyes, and she shook her head uncertainly. 'I can't imagine what you can possibly have to confide in me,' she told him, 'that you couldn't much more easily tell to your grandmother. But if you say you can't, and if it's really important to you, then——'

She shrugged, and Andrés was obviously anxious to have her support. 'It is important to me, Francesca; will you help me?'

'I'd rather hear what you want of me first,' Francesca told him, cautious as always when dealing with him, and Andrés thrust his hands into his pockets once more before he replied; taking his time now that it came to the point.

'Earlier, when we talked at dinner, you said that you would have sacrificed a great deal, even your claim to Tradaro's, for someone you loved,' he reminded her, and Francesca glanced across at him swiftly, her eyes wary. 'Do you remember that, Francesca?'

She nodded, frowning. 'Yes. Yes, I remember saying that.'

'And you meant it, *sí*?'

Francesca nodded. Her brain was buzzing with warning bells, but now that she thought she had an inkling of what his confidence concerned, it was hard to just turn away. 'I meant what I said,' she agreed.

The moon briefly hid behind a streamer of cloud and it was difficult to see his expression, only that his head was bent while he regarded the toe of one highly polished shoe. 'Will you also believe that I am prepared to give up my inheritance for something more worthwhile?' Andrés asked, and she caught her breath.

It was something along the lines she had expected, but Francesca had not been prepared to hear him say he would give up his right to Trader's Cay when he had gone to so much trouble to gain her share of it as well. 'I find that hard to believe,' she managed, and Andrés looked up.

'You find it hard to believe that I could fall in love?' he challenged.

Francesca shook her head slowly, wishing she could decide whether or not he was simply playing another one of his tricks, but he seemed perfectly serious and very earnest about it. 'I didn't say that, Andrés,' she denied, 'it's just that——'

'You find it difficult to trust me, *sí*?' He smiled ruefully, and just for a moment Francesca actually felt sympathy for him. Shrugging his shoulders, he seemingly accepted her mistrust as inevitable. 'I cannot blame you, Francesca,' he told her. 'But I had thought—it was because I thought you perhaps—cared for my father, that I hoped you would understand how I felt, and give me your help.'

Bypassing the question of her feelings for Antonio, Francesca looked at him curiously, still wary, though less so than she had been, if she had but realised it. Being in love was something she could understand, and it was possible even for someone like Andrés to be in love, she supposed. 'How could I possibly help you?' she asked. 'Surely if you're genuinely in love with this girl, whoever she is, your father wouldn't be unreasonable about you marrying her.'

He wasn't looking at her again, but down at his feet, one toe prodding the lush growth of fern that grew in the crevice of the path. 'I know that he would,' he said. 'You see, she lives in Madrid and she will not leave there to live in a place like Tradaro's.'

'I see.' Francesca remembered how unhappy his mother had been, according to Cecilia Morales, and she could sympathise with anyone who was confined to a small island when their taste was for city life. She could sympathise with Andrés too, although it would have seemed an unlikely thing to happen until this moment. 'I don't quite see——' she began, but Andrés cut her short, taking her hands and holding them firmly between his own.

'But you *can* help me, Francesca! Francesca *bonita*, you know how I feel and you will help me, *sí*? *Sí*?' He urged her to agree, and it was in something of a daze that Francesca agreed by nodding her head.

'But I don't quite see how,' she insisted. 'I can't *do* anything, Andrés. I could mention it to your father, but I don't really have any influence with him, whatever Señora Morales says.'

'Oh no, no, no!' Andres insisted hastily. 'Do not say one word to my father of this! I wish only to *see* her——'

'Doesn't she have a name?'

He looked at her blankly for a moment, then smiled. 'Mujer,' he said. '*Sí*, Mujer Desconocida.'

'Is it someone your family know?' she asked, and noticed that he frowned as if he did not like discussing the girl he professed to love.

'No,' he admitted with obvious reluctance. 'No, they do not know her, Francesca, but does that mean that I cannot love her? Help me to see her again, Francesca, *por favor*! I will return to Tradaro's, but Abuela and my father will not trust me to do this, and I shall most surely break my heart if I do not go!'

He looked so young and so earnest, pleading for a chance to see his girl-friend once more, and in her present mood it was easier for Francesca to sympathise with him. 'I'm not sure I ought to trust you either,' she told him in a last stand against his pleading. 'And I don't see how I can help, Andrés, honestly.'

He was studying the ground at his feet again and she could not see what was in his eyes, but he looked oddly appealing as he scuffed his toe over the rough paving. 'I do not like to ask such a thing of a woman,' he said with a curiously touching dignity, 'but I have no money, and I need money to get to Madrid. You have money, *sí*?'

'Yes.' Already her heart was pounding furiously when she considered the situation she might be getting herself into with Antonio, and surely Señora Morales would not sympathise with her in this instance. Yet it was well-nigh impossible to resist his appeal when he looked so very much like Antonio standing there in the moonlight. 'You *will* come back?' she insisted, and Andrés nodded urgently.

Leaning towards her, he clasped her hands in his and his eyes seemed to have an hypnotic effect, banishing her doubts. '*Por favor*, Francesca,' he whispered, and she heaved a great sigh of resignation.

'I shall probably be very, very sorry for it,' she told him with a rueful smile, 'but—yes, all right, I'll help you go and see your girl in Madrid. I'll—make some excuse for drawing so much money from the bank.'

'*Gracias*, oh, *gracias, gracias*!' He kissed her hands fervently, his lips soft and moist and surprisingly cool on her fingers. 'I shall leave in three days, with the *Sur Viento*!' He looked slightly uneasy when she frowned curiously at him. 'A schooner,' he explained, then immediately kissed her fingers again, his dark eyes beaming down at her. 'Oh,

Francesca, how happy you have made me!'

'I only hope——' Francesca began, but he cut her short, his expression anxious.

'Oh, Francesca, you will not now change your mind; you could not be so cruel!'

'I won't change my mind,' she promised, but wondered already, how she was going to explain it to Antonio. And assuredly it would be she who was called upon to explain, for Andrés would be far away.

CHAPTER EIGHT

FRANCESCA was not quite sure what she expected to happen, but in her heart she supposed she rather hoped Andrés would have second thoughts about visiting his girl-friend in Madrid. It had not been as easy as she anticipated getting the money either, but she had managed it somehow without arousing too much curiosity. She had, after all, her own independent fortune left her by her grandfather, and the only difficulty was in getting to the bank to withdraw such a sum without causing comment.

Having successfully achieved it, she sought to persuade Andrés to change his mind before she handed him the money, but it was quite clear that he had no intention of doing so if he could possibly help it. Ever since she had made him that rather rash promise of help, she had been unhappy about it, mostly, she admitted, on account of Antonio.

'Surely,' she pleaded when she gave Andrés the money while they walked in the garden one evening before dinner, 'if you explained to your father, he wouldn't try to stop you seeing the girl you love. He isn't heartless, Andrés, nor is he unreasonable. Couldn't you just ask him—see how he reacts?'

'I know exactly how he would react,' Andrés insisted, 'and I could not bear to have him stop me now. You have such a—a naïve view of him, Francesca. I have set my heart upon this trip, do not break your promise to me now, *por favor!*'

Francesca looked down at her clasped hands, assailed by any number of doubts, now that it was virtually too late to stop it. It did not matter to her personally if Andrés left the island for good, but she shrank from the fact that she had deliberately deceived Antonio to help him, and it was for that reason alone she sought to make him change his mind at the last moment.

Perhaps Andrés was right, and her view of Antonio was rather naïve, but she could not believe that he would deliberately deny his son a chance of happiness with the girl he loved. She looked so unhappy that most men, however young and selfish, would have been moved by her obvious anxiety to some extent. Not so Andrés, he was much too self-concerned.

'I—I don't know how I'm going to tell your father,' Francesca told him.

'Then do not tell him,' he suggested blandly, and she frowned.

'You might show a little more concern,' she scolded reproachfully. 'He's going to be furious when he finds out you've gone, Andrés, and I don't think I have the nerve to tell him that I actually helped you by paying your fare.'

'Then do not let him know you did,' Andrés insisted, and he eyed her for a moment warily. 'You would not betray me now by warning him, would you, Francesca?'

It was what she felt like doing, but she shrugged uneasily, disliking that term betrayal. 'I just hate deceiving him, that's all.'

Francesca tried not to notice the way his lip curled for a moment before he answered. 'So—sensitive, eh?'

'I'm just not devious by nature!' she said, finding the retort irresistible, and the way he smiled suggested that Andrés took the allusion as a compliment.

'The *Sur Viento* will put in early tomorrow morning,' he told her, 'and I shall go abroad just before she leaves. Whether or not you tell my father after that will not concern me because, as you know from experience, he will not trouble himself to come after me personally. Nor will it concern me whether or not you tell him that I had your assistance.'

'I wouldn't——'

'Ah, but I think you would, Francesca!' His dark eyes regarded her for a moment and she recognised the familiar glint of malice lurking in their depths—a fact that added to her uneasiness. 'I think you will not be able to help yourself,' Andrés went on confidently. 'You will tell him where I have gone, and also that you provided me with the necessary means to go, because you will feel compelled to do so. It will be foolish to make such a confession, but you will make it because you are rather a foolish girl, Francesca. Charming and very lovely, but foolishly honest!'

'And you don't give a damn what happens now that you've got your own way!' Francesca accused. She was trembling, her legs horribly weak suddenly as she tried to make excuses for herself, and for what she had done. There was something about him that set the warning bells ringing in her brain again, and she looked at him anxiously, praying that just this once he had not been devious. 'Andrés, you wouldn't— you wouldn't fool me, would you? Not in something like this? I mean, you *are* going back to Madrid to see your girl? You know I wouldn't have helped you otherwise.'

'I know it!'

'Then——'

'I am eternally grateful that you have such a romantic heart, Francesca.' A hint of a smile hovered around his mouth, but she could not detect mockery and she accepted it at face value for the moment. 'It is because you have—the soft spot?—for lovers that you have deceived my father to help me, sí? I know it, Francesca; let us hope that my father understands it too, eh?'

'Who is she—*what* is she, this Mujer Desconocida of yours?'

His eyes were shadowed and it was very hard to tell what was going on behind them, but that faint suggestion of smile still lingered about his mouth. 'She is—nobody, Francesca; just—a nobody.'

'Oh, I see. Someone your family wouldn't approve of?'

She thought of the sordid slum he had lived in while he was absent from home the last time, and wondered if he had a taste for low life that extended to his choice of a girlfriend. To have done what she had to make it possible for him to see a nice, decent girl would have been acceptable, but someone less desirable would make it much harder to justify herself to Antonio and Señora Morales.

'*Is* she someone they wouldn't approve of, Andrés?' she insisted.

'There is absolutely nothing for them to disapprove of, I promise you,' he said, and sounded so convincing she was bound to believe him.

'Then why not tell them——'

'Francesca, *por favor*!' He shook his head as if he despaired of her ever understanding. 'This is my secret for the moment, sí?' She nodded, willing to be convinced, and he hastened to assure her of his gratitude, although she would have as soon dispensed with verbal proof of it. 'You have helped me to return to Madrid, and for that I shall be indebted to you; although it is a debt that I cannot promise to repay for a very long time.'

'Oh no, please, there's no need to worry about that,' Francesca insisted hurriedly. 'Just as long as you come back to Trader's Cay when you've seen your girl, as you said you would, that's all.'

'Francesca *dulce*!' He took her hand and raised it to his lips, thick black lashes still holding his eyes from her. 'And now it is getting late, and you must go and prepare for dinner, eh?'

'What about you?'

She checked the time by her own wristwatch, then looked at him curiously, appalled to realise how hard it was for her to trust him. But Andrés was smiling, and once more he raised her fingers and kissed them, his lips light and cool, without fervour; which struck her as strange for a son of Antonio's.

'I have something that I must do before I can join you,' he told her. 'But it does not take so long for a man to prepare for dinner as it does a woman, hah?' He laughed and gave her fingers a final squeeze before letting them go. '*Adiós*, Francesca, and *muchas gracias*!'

He turned and went striding off along the path with a casual wave of his hand, and Francesca watched him until he turned the first corner and disappeared among the riot of shrubs and trees that crowded in, blaming herself for being so suspicious. Andrés was a young man in love, and by helping him she was simply furthering the cause of true love. It was something that Señora Morales would probably understand and forgive, even if Antonio didn't.

It was much less easy to feel justified in what she had done, Francesca found, when she had more time to dwell on it, and all the time she was dressing for dinner she went over and over that scene in the garden with Andrés. He had eventually convinced her that she was simply helping a young man in love, and yet something about his manner in retrospect rang warning bells in her brain.

No matter how urgently he had pleaded for her help in seeing his girl, she should not have allowed herself to be persuaded into keeping it a secret from his father. She owed him nothing except some moments of extreme discomfort, and yet she could never forget that he was Antonio's son. Had it not been that she was feeling so disturbingly emotional about Antonio that evening, she would never have allowed herself to be drawn into such a wild scheme, and the more she dwelt on that interview with Andrés just now, the more convinced she was that he had been laughing at her without openly doing so.

She was still plagued by misgivings when she came downstairs, and finding Antonio in sole possession of the *salon* seemed the last straw, so that she almost turned right around and went out again. He turned the moment she walked into the room, however, and held up the sherry bottle with an enquiring arch of one brow. She nodded acceptance, and inwardly regretted that evening dress was the exception rather than the rule, for she felt that a little additional glamour would have boosted her low morale.

'Isn't Andrés down yet?' she asked as she took her drink from him, and realised that by asking the obvious she had aroused his curiosity.

He would have no illusions concerning her relationship with his son, and she knew he would be trying to find a reason for her asking. 'As you can see, he is not,' he told her. Taking a sip from his glass, he quizzed her with curious blue eyes. 'Why, Francesca? You do not usually concern yourself with Andrés' whereabouts,' he pointed out when she blinked in confusion, and she took a hasty sip from her own glass.

'I—I just wondered, that's all.'

'Ah!'

It was the ensuing silence that brought her to the brink

of confession; that and the growing realisation that she could not go on deceiving him, whatever the cause. As Andrés had told her, she was almost foolishly honest, and particularly where Antonio was concerned. She took another hasty sip from her drink with the idea of boosting her courage, but swallowed too hastily and found herself coughing and desperately trying to catch her breath suddenly.

'*Cuidado, chica!* Not so quickly, ah?'

The hand that rubbed soothingly over her back was so unexpected that Francesca almost choked anew, and it was incredibly affecting being in such close contact with him again after the way he had been keeping his distance during the past couple of days. She was all but tucked under his arm, while he patted and soothed away the choking cough, and it was purely instinct that made her lean lightly against him.

Her cheeks were flushed and there were tears in her eyes, and she pursed her lips in an expression of relief when she eventually recovered, looking up at him briefly. His mouth was smiling, that small, almost secret smile that she knew so well, and his eyes had a deep dark warmth that was so like a caress that the effect of it shivered over her skin, bringing a startling awareness of his proximity. One arm still kept her close to his side, reminding her of the temptation there was in the pulsing heat of his body and the firm pressure of his hand on her back through the thin material of her dress.

'O.K.?'

He asked the question so gently that she merely nodded, having no breath to speak. Also it was incredibly difficult to meet his eyes, knowing how she had deceived him, something he was bound to notice. Although at the moment he appeared only curious rather than suspicious.

'You have enough breath now to talk?' he asked, and again she nodded agreement.

'I think so,' she said huskily.

'Then tell me what is troubling you, Francesca, eh?' he suggested, and shook his head firmly against her unspoken denial, while his hand still smoothed slowly back and forth across her shoulder blades, as if the motion was entirely automatic. 'Have you and Andrés had some kind of a disagreement? Is that it? Or has he been playing his dangerous tricks again?'

He looked so fierce when he said it that Francesca spoke up quickly. 'Oh no, no, nothing like that!' She wanted desperately to sustain that mood of gentle curiosity as long as possible, because she knew that the moment he heard what she had done, anger was inevitable. She was convinced he would never forgive her, and yet that innate honesty that Andrés had so obviously despised drove her on; courting disaster. 'Antonio, do you—do you know anything about a girl called—Mujer Desconocida?'

Antonio's first reaction was a blink of obvious surprise, and then he smiled. But it was the nature of his smile that Francesca found disturbing, for it suggested mockery as well as amusement, and very reluctantly she moved away from actual contact with him, though she did not go too far. Just far enough for her to be able to consider what she said without being distracted by his nearness.

'You are making a joke?' he suggested, and Francesca looked at him more warily than ever as he thrust one hand into the pocket of his jacket.

She was assailed again by her earlier misgivings, and wished Andrés would hurry up and put in an appearance, so that it could not be said that she had gone behind his back to betray him. 'I'm not joking,' she told Antonio. 'Surely you can say whether or not you know her.'

'A—*mujer desconocida*, you say?'

Something in his voice made small hairs prickle all along the nape of her neck, and her reply was tautly defensive because of it. 'All right, maybe my accent isn't very good, but that's what it sounded like to me! I'm just curious to know who she is, that's all!'

'Understandably!' His continued amusement puzzled her, and she realised that only when she looked at him directly and he noticed the anxiety in her eyes, did he sober a little. Setting his glass down on the sideboard, he turned back to face her, scanning her flushed features with a slight frown. 'Your pronunciation is almost faultless,' he told her quietly. 'But in what connection has this—*mujer desconocida* been mentioned, Francesca?'

Francesca shifted uneasily, anxiously aware of something unexpected about to be sprung on her, and she put down her own glass still half full, then glanced at the door, willing Andrés to appear. 'I—I heard the name,' she murmured, and moistened her lips with the tip of her tongue. There was little else she could do but go on when Antonio's speculative gaze rested on her so quizzically. 'She's—Andrés told me about her. She's his girl-friend.'

'Hah!'

The fervour of his realisation startled her for a moment, but he was still smiling and she took heart from that. Maybe at any moment now his mood would change, and she felt a surge of anguish at the very thought of it happening. 'He—he loves her,' she informed him huskily, and again flicked the tip of her tongue across dry lips before she went on. 'He told me that he loves her and he longs to see her again. She lives in Madrid, so I suppose he met her when he was living there with his grandparents.'

'No, no, *nena*!' His smile was teasing but gentle, and his voice soft, lulling her wariness and bringing a momentary glow of warmth to ease her heart. 'Andrés was teasing you! If your Spanish was not so limited, you would know that *mujer desconocida* means simply—an unknown woman.'

Francesca stared at him and her eyes were blank with

dismay. Her heart thudded wildly in near panic, for she realised that she had been fooled even more thoroughly than she had ever dreamed she could be. In a welter of chaotic emotions she pressed on, seeking to discover the full extent of Andrés deceit. 'Is there a ship——' Her tongue flew over parched lips as her voice dried up, and she rolled both hands into tight fists in her anxiety. 'Is there a schooner called the *Sur Viento*, due to call here in the morning?'

Francesca had little conscience about betraying the whole scheme now, and, warned by her obvious distress, Antonio no longer smiled. Instead the first glimmer of suspicion showed in the slight narrowing of his eyes. It was a familiar prelude and she prepared to face his wrath, feeling small and horribly vulnerable as she waited for it to happen.

'The *Sur Viento* was due to leave Tradaro's about half an hour ago,' Antonio told her in a cool flat voice. 'I have no reason to think she did not sail on time.'

'Oh no!' It was a muted, whispered plea, and a useless one, Francesca knew, and Antonio's gaze still held hers firmly, darkly suspicious even before he knew the reason for her stricken expression. 'I—I didn't realise. I should have known; I should have remembered; I should have——' She threw up her hands in despair, choking on the recrimination she poured on to her own head.

There was a kind of stillness about Antonio, a kind of calm before the storm, she guessed, and knew that the anger she had anticipated was going to be even harder to face because she did not even have the cause of romance to offer in her own defence. So thoroughly had Andrés deceived her.

'I assume there is a reason for your questions,' he said. 'Your interest in an unknown woman and your mention of the *Sur Viento*.' His eyes were dark and compelling as they sought to probe the truth from her. 'Enlighten me, Francesca, *por favor*!'

Too close to tears, Francesca put her hands to her mouth and closed her eyes, shaking her head back and forth despairingly. Her instincts had warned her not to trust Andrés, but she had allowed herself to be swayed by her own romantic notions, enabling him to use her as a means of procuring him the funds he needed.

'Francesca?' Warning sounded in the voice that roused her from contemplation of her own folly, and long hard fingers closed around her wrists, pulling away her hands and exposing her look of despair. 'What has happened? And do not deny that nothing has, *niña*, for I will not be convinced!' He glanced over his shoulder at the door of the *salón*, much as she had done herself only a few moments before, then his grip on her tightened until she caught her breath to protest, only to be forestalled. 'I will not trouble myself to look for Andrés,' Antonio said harshly. 'I suspect he is no longer on the island!'

Francesca felt the bruising force of his hands and knew that it was an expression of anguish; the only one he would make, for anger would be his way of relieving his feelings at the departure of his son. It would have been hard for her to bear in any circumstances, but knowing how she had contributed to it was unendurable, and Francesca pulled away from him, tears flowing unchecked down her cheeks as she sought to go past him and out of the room.

'No!' He caught her wrist again as she passed him and swung her round to face him, a burning fierceness in his eyes. 'You knew.' The way he spoke, so quietly and resignedly made it worse, and she caught a sob in her throat when he looked directly at her. '*How* did you know, Francesca? Why would he confide in you and not in his grandmother? Why you, Francesca?'

Her voice seemed choked in her throat, and her legs barely able to support her, but escape was impossible. 'Because—because I'm an idiot!' she declared in a trembling voice and sparing herself nothing. 'Because I'm stupid and gullible, and ready to believe anything anyone tells me, even someone as devious and underhand as Andrés! Why shouldn't he confide in me when he knew I was in the right mood and silly enough to fall in with his plan?'

Antonio released her wrists and turned to refill his glass as if he was completely unaware of what he was doing, and by now the desire to escape at any cost had passed. Francesca stood watching him, her tears flowing unheeded and her brain trying in vain to come to terms with the wild insistence of her emotions.

She loved him and she had helped his son to deceive him. The two facts were inescapable and incompatible, and she could not imagine where she could go from there. She hated Andrés with a fury she would never have believed herself capable of at one time, and mostly she knew it was because he had made her the means of hurting his father.

While she stood there, silent and vulnerable and entirely without defence, Antonio turned and looked at her again. She could not see the expression in his eyes because he kept the lids half closed and the thickness of black lashes concealed the anger and despair she knew must be there.

'Tell me,' he said quietly, and she bit hard into her lower lip to stop herself from whimpering because he wasn't raging at her.

'He—he told me that he had a girl in Madrid; a girl he was in love with and *had* to see again.'

'And you believed him?'

'I believed him.' For once she was not roused to anger by the tone of his voice, and his silence in the moments that followed gave her the courage to go on. 'I know he loves Madrid and he loves—he told me he loved a girl who lives there. I know he isn't really an island man like you, Señora Morales told me so, but he *did* promise me he'd come back to Trader's Cay when he'd seen——'

'This girl who does not exist!'

Her colour rose and Francesca shook her head. 'I was a bit naïve about that,' she confessed, 'but he was very convincing.'

'My son has the gift of being very convincing,' Antonio allowed, and the note of re_ignation in his voice was very hard to take.

'I'm sorry, Tonio.'

It was difficult to believe he was simply standing there and accepting the situation so passively, when she expected a tirade of anger. But it had slipped her mind for the moment that he did not yet know of her own part in Andrés' latest disappearance. 'What I find puzzling is why he spoke of it to you,' Antonio said after a moment or two, and sounded rather more as if he was musing over it for his own benefit. 'You were not friends; you did not even like one another it seemed to me, and yet he confided in you matters that he kept from me and from his grandmother.'

'You—you would have tried to stop him,' Francesca ventured huskily. 'That was what he was afraid of.'

'I certainly do not wish him to go to Madrid,' Antonio agreed, 'and nor does his grandmother, because there is always the possibility he will not return.'

'And that matters to you.'

She had no need to make it a question, and Antonio looked at her steadily. 'Of course it matters to me, Francesca. He is my only son; my only child, and there is Tradaro's——'

'Is that the only reason he matters to you?' She had spoken without stopping to think, because he had made the Morales inheritance the reason for wanting his son back. But she knew it wasn't the only reason, and when the look in his eyes reproached her she hastily looked away, whispering her regret.

'I'm sorry.'

'How could he raise the fare to Madrid?'

He was musing again, and she caught her breath when he looked at her suddenly and narrowed his eyes. What she saw there made her press the back of one hand to her mouth while her eyes made a desperate appeal. 'I—I believed him, Tonio,' she whispered in a small choked voice. 'I'd never have helped him otherwise! Please, *please* believe that!'

'*Santa Madre de Dios!*' he breathed, and his head drooped, shaking back and forth in despair. 'He has made a sneak and and a liar of you too!'

'Tonio!'

Try as she would, there seemed nothing she could say in her own defence and, crying uncontrollably, she turned and hurried from the room. At the moment she could think of only one way out of a situation that had suddenly become intolerable. She had vowed never to give up her claim to Trader's Cay, but in the present circumstances she saw herself with little alternative. Antonio wanted Trader's Cay and she wanted Antonio more than anything in the world; only one of them, as she saw it, stood the remotest chance of getting what they wanted.

Francesca had gone without her dinner the previous evening rather than face what she knew must be an ordeal. She simply could not bring herself to sit at table with Antonio and Señora Morales knowing how they must feel about her in their hearts, even if politeness on the *señora*'s part had precluded an open quarrel.

But remaining in her room could at best be only a temporary refuge; an opportunity to gather her wits and try to think clearly about what she could do. Sooner or later she must go downstairs and face them, but it was horribly nerve-racking anticipating Antonio's reaction, when she could so easily recall him shaking his head despairingly while he designated her a sneak and a liar for her part in his son's scheme.

When she first woke to the inevitable warm sunny morning, it seemed scarcely possible that she had slept after all, and even less credible that she had woken feeling ravenously hungry. But whatever happened, she was young and healthy, and she had gone a long time without food, and her system clamoured for sustenance. She listened to Antonio go past on his way downstairs, but made no endeavour to get up until she was certain he would have left the house. He would be gone for at least a couple of hours, and while he was absent she might have the opportunity of talking with Señora Morales.

Not that she anticipated the older woman's complete forgiveness, but at least she felt confident of a hearing, whereas she doubted if Antonio would even bother to acknowledge her existence. She had cried for a long time last night before she eventually got to sleep, but she was still no nearer to finding an alternative solution to the one she had made on impulse, immediately after she left Antonio in the *salón*.

She could leave on the first available boat; the little Jamaican skipper who had first brought her to Trader's Cay was due in in a couple of days' time, and she hadn't really very much to pack. Her presence made very little difference to the running of the estate, for Antonio had managed perfectly well before she arrived, and she could leave it to their lawyers to sell her share to him. It was, after all, what he had wanted all along, so he was hardly likely to raise any objections; and he would, she had little doubt, forget her far more readily and quickly than she would him.

She bit her lip hard as she came downstairs, and it occurred to her that if she waited for breakfast she would more than likely be sharing the table not only with Señora Morales, but with Antonio as well. With that in mind, she paid her first and only visit to the kitchen, surprising the kitchen staff into regarding her with a hint of suspicion.

They concurred readily enough with her request for something to eat, however, and she tucked into coffee, bread rolls and honey on the cool blue-tiled porch, in solitary silence.

Her hunger appeased, she went along to the *salón* to await Cecilia Morales' appearance, and was blessedly relieved to be greeted so warmly, when she had expected disapproval. 'Francesca!' Cecilia looked around the big room, for a sign of her son presumably, and not seeing him looked vaguely unhappy. 'My dear child, are you unwell?'

'Oh no, *señora*—thank you.'

'But you had no dinner; you must be very hungry, I will ask——'

'Oh, no, please, Señora Morales, there's no need!' Francesca smiled faintly, but was well aware that her eyes were still red-rimmed and puffy, making it obvious that she had cried for hours over the hopelessness of her situation. 'I—I begged something from the kitchen when I came down earlier, and I'm fine now, really.'

It was quite clear that there was much to puzzle the older woman as she sat down facing her. Her fine black brows were drawn and her dark eyes troubled. 'You should not have missed your dinner last night, Francesca,' she told her. 'There was really no need, and I cannot imagine why you did so.'

Francesca's hands folded and unfolded restlessly as she offered an explanation she had little hope would satisfy her kindly inquisitor. 'I just didn't feel like eating, *señora*.'

'Well, it was very foolish of you, and I had difficulty in preventing Tonio from coming upstairs to fetch you. I knew you would not wish him to do that, but he was very concerned that you missed your meal.'

'I'm surprised he even bothered himself about me,' said Francesca, keeping a firm grip on her self-control. 'I—I just couldn't face him, or you, knowing how I'd let Andrés fool me.'

Dark eyes traversed her unhappy face, and Francesca wondered if she knew the full extent of her misdeeds, or if Antonio had omitted some of it in the telling. Señora Morales was treating her far more gently than she felt entitled to expect in the circumstances, and it somehow made her feel much worse.

'It was surely no reason for hiding yourself away in your room, child,' Señora Morales chided gently. 'Going without food will not bring Andrés home again, nor will it do you any good.'

It was hard to remain controlled when she was being treated with such kindness, and Francesca clasped her hands tightly together while she sought for words. 'Did—didn't Antonio tell you what I did?' she ventured, and Señora Morales nodded slowly. 'All of it, *señora*?'

There was reproach in her eyes when Francesca glanced at her briefly, but no real condemnation, and she was very tempted to cry like a baby in sheer self-pity. 'You were very foolish, *niña*,' she was told, 'and I cannot understand how you allowed yourself to be so—misguided, when you know how strongly Tonio feels about Andrés remaining here on Tradaro's.'

'I know.' Remembering how tangled her emotions had been on that particular evening, Francesca shook her head and bit anxiously into her bottom lip while she pondered on her explanation. 'But it seemed so hard on Andrés when he was so anxious to see his girl again. He said he loved her and that he wanted to see her again very much, and he explained that you and Tonio would never agree to him going for fear he didn't come back. I—I knew that was true.'

'And yet you still helped him? To disobey his father?'

Francesca's hands were restless on her lap as she remembered her own earlier reaction to disobedience against Antonio's ruling. 'I hate that word, obey,' she confessed 'It suggests an—unreasoning demand made on someone against their will, and I tried to tell Andrés that I didn't believe Tonio was like that. Then I remembered how—how insistent he can be when he has his mind set on something, and I thought he might *not* let Andrés go and see his girl after all. I was misguided, as you said, *señora,* but I was in a—a curious mood that evening and I suppose I was more gullible than usual, more open to persuasion.'

Señora Morales smiled faintly. 'And my grandson can be very persuasive,' she allowed.

Francesca was grateful for her understanding, but ready to admit her own weakness. 'I was in a mood to be persuaded,' she said.

The *señora* nodded. 'I realise, of course, that Tonio had been unforgivably harsh towards you, but he spoke without thought, child, as we all do on occasion. And he would have followed you and made his peace, if you had allowed him to.'

'I know.'

'Why then did you not allow him to make his peace, instead of seeking such revenge?' the *señora* asked sadly, and Francesca stared at her for a moment in blank disbelief.

Then it began to dawn on her what Cecilia thought was behind her helping Andrés to leave, and she shook her head with increasing urgency as she denied it. 'Oh but, *señora,* you surely don't—you can't believe I helped Andrés just because Tonio lost his temper with me and was abrupt! I was upset, I admit, but you surely can't think I'd be so—so spiteful as to deliberately strike back at him through Andrés!' From her expression it was clear that it was exactly the motive Cecilia Morales had attributed to her action, and she shook her head slowly in reproach. 'I wouldn't,' she insisted huskily. 'I was a fool; a complete idiot to be taken in as I was, but I wouldn't take revenge like that, you must know I wouldn't!'

'It seemed unlike you to fall in with any plan of Andrés',' his grandmother insisted, but clearly realised she had misjudged her.

'If I hadn't believed he had a girl in Madrid, and that he loved her and wanted to see her again, I'd never have helped him,' Francesca told her. 'But I was——' She shrugged uneasily, recalling how emotional she had been that fateful evening. 'I sympathised with him being in love, and I didn't like to think of him being forbidden to see his girl, as he assured me would happen because you and Tonio wouldn't trust him to come back. But he promised me he *would* come back, *señora*, and idiot that I am, I believed him.'

'You had a tender heart for young love?' Cecilia Morales suggested, and recalling that Andrés had said much the same thing, Francesca nodded. 'I should have known that you would not do such a thing to punish Tonio for the way he spoke to you, and I am sorry I misjudged you, child. Can you forgive me?'

'Of course I will,' Francesca assured her unhesitatingly. But she thought Antonio would be less easily placated, and believing it she pressed on with what she had to say before he put in an appearance. There was little sense in prolonging the agony and, since she had firmly made up her mind, it was better to have it all cut and dried so that Señora Morales could perhaps be persuaded to break the news to him. 'I—I came to a decision last night, *señora*, and I'd—I'd rather like to tell you about it first, if you'll bear with me.'

Clearly her companion was not altogether happy about becoming her confidante; perhaps because she suspected what she had to say concerned Antonio in some way, and she preferred to remain uninvolved in her son's personal affairs. Nevertheless she nodded consent. 'Naturally, if you wish to confide in me, Francesca.'

Francesca looked at the hands clasped tightly together in

her lap rather than look at her, and she chose each word carefully, unwilling to give the wrong impression. 'I gave a lot of thought to my situation here last night, *señora*, and I've decided to do what Antonio has wanted me to do ever since I arrived. I've always turned it down whenever he's suggested it, but now——' She used her hands to express the sense of helplessness she felt. 'I believe it would be in everyone's best interests if I left Trader's Cay and went back to England as soon as possible.'

'Francesca!'

She clasped her hands so tightly that her fingers pressed into their backs and showed the fine bones, taut and fragile-looking. 'I shall go with Captain Leroy when he calls the day after tomorrow, and go back by the same route I came. Then when I get back I'll instruct my solicitors to arrange the sale of my share of the estate to Tonio for a reasonable price.' There was pain in her voice when she thought of leaving it all behind, and especially of never seeing Antonio again, and a bruised, hurt look in her eyes that she managed to conceal with lowered lashes. 'It won't really make up for deceiving him as I did, nor will it bring his son back, but it might help to ease the hurt a bit; and maybe Andrés will think it more worthwhile coming back for the whole island instead of only a half-share.'

Señora Morales actually looked shocked, and her head was shaking back and forth in disbelief, her eyes blank with dismay. 'Oh no, no, Francesca, you cannot do this! You cannot give up what my dear Francisco was so anxious for you to have! Nor will Tonio listen to such an idea, I am sure!'

But there was a set look on Francesca's unhappy face that suggested she knew better. 'Tonio will be only too glad to know that I've seen the light at last, and that he need no longer play nursemaid to me,' she insisted. Somehow she managed a small unsteady laugh, but it suggested tears rather than amusement. 'I think you'll find that he's more than willing to accept the offer, *señora*.'

'But what of you, child?'

'Me?' Again that faint, shivery laughter fluttered uncertainly into being. 'Oh, I shan't be sorry to get back to the normality of life in England. This is a little too—exotic for me.'

Cecilia Morales was obviously dazed by the speed of events, and scarcely believed what was happening. 'But only the other evening you said that you wished to spend the rest of your life here,' she recalled.

'Did I?' Francesca remembered very well making the claim, and she had meant it seriously. Only now she could see how impossible it was going to be, living in such close proximity to Antonio when her emotions were so deeply and hopelessly involved. She faced the fact that she was going to love him for the rest of her life, but in his heart she thought Antonio would always remember that she had given his son the means to leave Trader's Cay, perhaps for good. 'I'm certain I couldn't stay here for the rest of my life, Señora Morales, I'm far too much of a—a fish out of water. No, it will have to be England for me, and the familiar faces and things, and the sooner the better! A quick, clean break!'

She dared not go on because her voice felt choked in her throat, and she felt certain she was going to start crying again very soon. There was a look of gentle speculation in Cecilia Morales' eyes for a moment as she regarded her, then she shook her head. 'Are there not familiar things here that you will miss, Francesca?' she asked, and Francesca pressed her hands even more closely together.

So many things had become familiar in the comparatively short time she had been on her tropical island, and there was so much she would miss. The sun, the scents and colours of the exotic trees and flowers that surrounded her, and the sense of being her own mistress, of looking around and knowing that this paradise was at least half hers. And the mornings when she rode out with Antonio and he turned that enquiring and slightly mocking gaze on her as they started out.

'Francesca, you do not have to leave.' Cecilia Morales' quiet voice intruded into her thoughts, and she raised her head without looking directly at the speaker. 'Tonio does not blame you for Andrés going, and your going will not bring him back again. Can you not see, child, that giving up all that your grandfather left to you will not make any difference to the way this matter resolves itself?'

Francesca looked down at the hands on her lap, and restless fingers plucked at the skirt of her dress while she spoke. 'It—it will make a difference to me, *señora*,' she insisted in a thin, uncertain voice that she did her best to control. 'I don't want to stay on—I—I *can't* stay on because——' She got to her feet suddenly and brushed down her skirt with shaking hands. 'I'd be very grateful if you'd tell Tonio what I've decided,' she said. 'I'm sure you'll find he's perfectly happy with the idea of buying my half of Trader's Cay, it's what he's always wanted. And I'd sooner it was over quickly, now I've made up my mind.'

Cecilia drew herself up and for a moment she appeared very much the Spanish matriarch with her back straight and her head high. 'If you wish to offer your share of Tradaro's to Antonio, Francesca,' she said, 'you will have to make it in person or through another agent. I decline to act as your go-between because I am not in favour of it.'

It was the most formal speech Francesca had ever heard her make, and it put the onus firmly with her. It made a personal confrontation with Antonio inevitable, and that was something she wished to avoid at all costs. 'Please, Señora Morales,' she pleaded. 'I—I can't—I'd much rather you told him. I don't want to have to——'

'Then he must remain in ignorance!' Cecilia Morales declared firmly. But it was a firmness that was not long in yielding to her more usual kindness, and she shook her head slowly at Francesca's look of appeal. 'Oh, Francesca, my child,' she said softly, 'do you think I do not know why you wish to run so far away?'

Heart pounding wildly in the fear of discovery, Francesca turned her head swiftly when someone closed a door somewhere. It was getting close to nine-thirty and the last person she wanted to meet at the moment was Antonio coming in for breakfast. 'I'll tell him myself,' she gabbled breathlessly as she turned to go. 'But later!'

At any moment she expected to see him, and she went hurrying across the hall, hoping to be safely out of sight before Antonio appeared. Back in her room where she could think over the latest turn of events, but seeing no less need to do as she had said she would.

CHAPTER NINE

FRANCESCA suspected it was because she wanted to bring matters to a head that Señora Morales had spoken to her son, for Francesca herself had still not said a word to him about her departure. At the same time next day she would be already on her way in Captain Leroy's schooner, on the first leg of her journey back to England, and she had until now hoped against hope that his mother would break the news to Antonio.

Not that she had any doubt about his relief when he heard it, but she was less certain about her own emotions when it came to facing the fact of not seeing him again. She was unhappy, and anyone seeing her face to face would realise it. Antonio with his shrewd insight would quite probably come to the same conclusion as his mother had, and it was the idea of his knowing how she felt about him that made her feel sick with panic at the thought of facing him *tête-à-tête*.

'Madre tells me that you have something to say to me,' he said immediately after lunch the following day.

Francesca looked anxiously across at Señora Morales, but the older woman was already leaving the *salón* and carefully avoided her glance. Quite clearly Antonio was a little on edge and he sat on one end of the brocaded settee, lighting a long cigar before regarding her with disturbing directness through the ensuing smoke.

'Well, Francesca?' he prompted, so gently that it was almost her undoing.

Sitting on the very edge of her chair and very obviously ill at ease, she sought desperately for a place to begin, rubbing her hands over and over one another restlessly meanwhile. 'Have—have you heard anything from Andrés?' she ventured after a moment or two, and blinked in surprise when he nodded.

'He has telephoned.'

'From Madrid?'

It was hard to believe he was far away in that very different world, but Antonio was nodding agreement. 'Naturally, he had sufficient funds to fly direct.'

She quickly avoided his eyes again, her fingers more restless than ever 'Is he—all right?'

'Of course.' He concealed his expression with a cloud of pungent cigar smoke before he enlarged on it. 'He is staying with his maternal grandparents and very pleased with himself. Also,' he went on, and was clearly finding it hard to believe, 'he appears to be actually sorry for involving you.'

Francesca pleated the hem of her dress absently. 'That's something,' she suggested.

'He was, in fact, informative.' Francesca waited for him to

go on, but apparently he realised that they had strayed from the matter she wanted to talk about, and he extended one large hand invitingly. 'But you have something you wished to tell me?'

Now that it came to it, it was even harder than she had anticipated, and Francesca swallowed hard. 'I—I wanted to tell you—I have to tell you that——' She cleared her throat nervously and put a hand to her mouth. Bright blue eyes regarded her steadily through a haze of smoke, but he said nothing, only watched her with that unnerving steadiness. 'I—I thought about it for a long time, and I've decided to go home—to England.'

Just for a second he stared, and it dawned on her that he really had had no idea what she meant to tell him. There was a curious stillness about him for several seconds, then he leaned forward and knocked the ash from the end of his cigar, looking at what he was doing rather than at her. 'I see.' He took an interminable time getting his cigar to his liking, and Francesca slid a moistening tongue over her lips during the silence that followed. 'May I ask why?'

'Because I think it's time I did.' She tried to sound convincing but felt she was not making a very good job of it. 'I don't really belong here, and I think it would be better all round if I went back to the kind of life I'm more used to. The kind of people I'm used to.'

'That is to say that you do not care for our kind of people?' he suggested quietly, and Francesca hastened to deny it.

'Oh no, not at all! I like the people here and I've been very happy!'

'But you prefer to leave?'

'Yes.' She clasped her hands even more tightly, praying she could come through this nerve-racking interview without crying like an idiot and giving the game away. 'I—I just think it would be better all round if I go home, that's what it amounts to. I'll see my solicitor when I get back and he can arrange for you to buy my half of Trader's Cay.' Somehow she managed to very faintly smile in an attempt to defeat the tears that threatened. 'I—I promise not to make a profit at your expense, you can have it for less than market price.'

'I shall not,' Antonio assured her flatly. 'I have no desire to cheat you simply because you are conscience-stricken about Andrés.' When she looked up quickly to deny it, he held her wavering gaze until it dropped again, then went on, still in the same quiet almost matter-of-fact voice. 'There's no need for it, Francesca. I have faced the fact that not only is my son an adult with a mind of his own, but that he will never settle here. He would have found some excuse for returning to Madrid, either now or later. It makes little difference.'

Francesca caught the hurt in his voice and in his eyes before he hid it from her. And it was hard to believe he did not hold her at least partly responsible for speeding Andrés on his way, when he might have had him for a few more years at least. 'He tried so hard to get rid of me,' she ventured. 'And I can't understand why it mattered so much if he wasn't interested in the island coming to him eventually.'

'Eventually,' Antonio echoed, and again tapped ash from his cigar rather than look at her. 'Andrés does not like to wait for anything, and I am not yet an old man, as he has pointed out to me. Nor was he content to inherit only half of Tradaro's.'

'Then perhaps he'll come back,' she suggested, 'when you have the whole of the island again.'

'Perhaps,' he said, but seemed so unmoved by the possibility that Francesca wondered if he really had given up all hope of his son eventually taking over Trader's Cay from him.

'I—I don't know how long it will take. To settle the sale and everything,' she explained when he looked puzzled. Her voice was oddly light and breathless, for her heart hammered hard as she faced the prospect of the dream she had had of Trader's Cay as a paradise island being all over in only a matter of hours from then. 'I'm leaving with Captain Leroy tomorrow,' she went on. 'I'm sure he'll find room for me if I ask him nicely.'

His blue eyes regarded her for a moment, but it was impossible to tell what went on behind them for the thickness of black lashes. 'I am sure he will,' Antonio agreed. He continued to look at her and she found the scrutiny more disturbing than ever she had before, because she knew she was going to remember so much about him when she could no longer see him every day. 'You will be glad to return to England, of course,' he said. 'It is your home.'

'Yes. Yes, of course.'

He startled her by getting to his feet suddenly and she looked up at him, almost desperate to keep him with her for as long as possible. 'I assume you have told me all you wished to,' he said, and glanced at his wristwatch. 'If so then I will go and see Perez.' He smiled faintly, a small bitter smile that did not warm his eyes as his smiles had once done. 'Andrés was not the most reliable worker I had,' he said, 'but I shall miss his help with the more mundane tasks.'

'Oh, but if there's anything I can do!' Francesca got up from her chair and spoke up quickly. 'Couldn't I do whatever it is, just as well as Andrés?'

Antonio said nothing for a moment, but his eyes sought to hold her wavering gaze with a disturbing intensity for a moment. 'No, thank you,' he said, quietly but firmly. 'The running of Tradaro's need not concern you any longer; I can manage. *Hasta luego*, Francesca.'

Such rapid and complete exclusion from the affairs of the

island was unexpected, and for a moment or two after he had left her Francesca stood in the same spot, looking and feeling very small and lost. Quite clearly, having got what he wanted, Antonio no longer saw any need to bother about her, and as she walked across the *salón* she felt very close to tears again.

Dinner that evening was an ordeal and Francesca did not know how she got through it. And breakfast the following morning was no less traumatic, for it brought home to her the full force of what it was going to mean leaving behind a life style she had grown happily accustomed to.

When she bade her goodbye, Señora Morales was very obviously affected, and she hugged and kissed her, her dark eyes shiny with emotion. Antonio was to see her off at the pier so that his goodbye was made in public; very formal and proper, his features composed into the same stern and discouraging expression Francesca had noticed the day of her arrival.

When she offered him her hand to shake, however, he did raise it to his lips for a brief second, pressing his lips lightly to her fingers. At once her pulse responded, the blood pounding wildly through her heart until she felt it would stop beating altogether, and it was only with a great deal of self-control that she managed to stop herself changing her mind there and then about going.

The same dark faces watched her departure that had watched her arrive, and clearly most of them were sad and puzzled by her going. They were friendly people and she liked them; she did not want to leave them nor her island, it was all too precious and familiar to her. The sheds looming like yawning monsters on the searing hot concrete, and the mop-headed palms behind the functional yards; even the little pier where the schooner was tied up, it was all so much the same as she remembered it that first day.

Even the captain's wide friendly smile as he welcomed her aboard in sing-song island English. She remembered feeling a moment of panic at the thought of being left alone when the schooner departed and left her behind on that occasion. Yet she felt more wretched now that it was making for the open sea again and taking her away from her precious island.

A freighter stood off in the deeps, and a long boat scuttled busily across the water, but she saw them only through a haze of tears that the captain was discreet enough not to notice. They were skimming around the tip of Trader's Cay when he put a hand to his eyes and stared for a moment, then walked smartly astern, shouting orders as he went. Too steeped in her own unhappiness to be interested, Francesca stood in the bow, gazing down at the froth of white water that curled back in a ruffle of feathers before the cleaving prow.

Then it dawned on her that they had stopped and were tossing gently on the light swell. An engine sounded somewhere and men's voices, and after a second or two Francesca straightened slowly and raised her head, her ears attuned to a familiar voice, yet unable to believe she was not mistaken.

The rapid, thudding beat of her heart almost choked her, and she heard the captain laugh, his sing-song voice advancing, accompanied by the pad of footsteps on the deck and coming forward. She was out of sight, standing where she was, and hidden by the bulk of the wheelhouse, but she could hear the voices and there was no mistaking the deep quiet tone of the second man.

'You sayin' she's your woman, M'st Morales?'

'I am,' Antonio's unmistakable voice asserted firmly. 'And I want her back, Captain!'

Above the racing, deafening thud of her heart Francesca heard the little captain chuckle delightedly; he was obviously enjoying the incident enormously, and Francesca turned swiftly to face the two men as they came into sight. The captain's bright dark eyes beamed wickedly and he indicated her standing there with a waving hand, before turning away.

Antonio stood on the gently rolling deck with his feet slightly apart and his arms hung loosely at his sides. His hair was windblown and fell across his brow and briefly he ran impatient fingers through it, but his eyes never left her face. It was his eyes that Francesca found so affecting, for they were bright and gleaming and they had never looked more deeply blue, but behind the glint of determination lurked an unexpected hint of appeal, and it was that which proved so irresistible.

'Francesca.'

It was almost a question, and Francesca responded to it unhesitatingly. Without a word she walked over to him and looked up into the face she had feared she would never see again after those few moments on the pier just now. 'You—you came to fetch me back?' she asked, and her voice was uncontrollably husky.

He had said he never would appeal to anyone to come home, and she still found it hard to believe he was doing so now; to her of all people. 'I came to *ask* you to come back to me,' Antonio corrected her softly, but he already knew the answer when he reached and took the hand she offered.

In a daze she made the dizzying transition from schooner to long boat without a moment of fear, then the engine started and she was standing on unsteady legs as they skimmed over the water. She had scarcely had time to draw breath, and she turned swiftly when Antonio cut the engine while they were still some distance from Trader's Cay, her heart racing breathlessly with anticipation, apprehension? She could not tell.

The boat bobbed lightly on the surface of the shimmering ocean while he came around to where she stood beside the engine casing. Francesca was trembling and her legs felt barely capable of supporting her, as he placed a hand either side of her on the casing, legs braced against the rocking motion of the boat. She was vaguely aware that the schooner was still in sight, off to her right, but there was the silent privacy of the ocean around them, and an almost choking urgency in her heart beat.

Briefly she raised her eyes and met the bright blue gaze that seemed to see right through her. 'You—you told the captain I was your——'

She could not quite bring herself to say it, and she caught a glimpse of his smile before she lowered her eyes again. 'Do you wish me to prove it to his satisfaction, Francesca?' he challenged softly, and she nodded, thrilling to his possessive claim to her.

He drew her into his arms, not forcefully, but with a slowness that was more exciting than force, and his hands persuaded her closer yet. The first touch of his body was a flame that kindled the wild, untameable sensations she remembered so vividly, and she lifted her arms, clasping them behind his dark head and sighing deeply as she drew it down towards her. Her eyes closed, yielding and defence-less.

The touch of his mouth was warm and persuasive and lightly coaxing until she parted her lips, then he took fierce possession of them, plunging deeply into the soft eagerness of her mouth. There was a pulsing virility in him that charged like fire, a fire she responded to because there was nothing else she could do, and she clung to him, pressed close, so close it was like being a part of him.

His feet were still planted firmly apart on the deck, but her own slid on the worn planks, and he gathered her to him more closely still, pressing his lips to the vulnerable curve of her nape when she leaned her face to the warmth of his chest. Murmuring in mingled English and Spanish, his voice was muffled by wind-tossed red hair, and he brushed it back with light gentle fingers.

'You must have known how I love you, *mi enamorada*,' he murmured, kissing her neck and throat and the tip of her ear. 'Why did you leave me, *mi pichon*?'

Francesca raised her head, meeting the bright, burningly expressive blue eyes directly. She remembered how Ana Morales had played a secondary role to his love of Trader's Cay, and just for a second she felt a twinge of apprehension. She would stay with him no matter if he required the same of her, but it was not a situation she would find easy to live with.

'You feared that if I asked you to marry me it would be because I wished to regain the whole of Tradaros?' he suggested softly, and she made a barely perceptible nod. 'Oh *mi amada*, how much my son has to answer for!' His lips pressed lightly to her brow and she rubbed her cheek on the warm softness of his shirt. 'And yet it was he who made me come for you when you would have deserted me.'

Lifting her head, Francesca frowned at him curiously. 'Andrés?'

'*Sí, niña*. When he called Madre after he arrived in Madrid, he told her that you were in love with me and suggested that you were a means of providing Tradaro's with more sons to carry on the tradition.' He saw the colour flood into her face and kissed her fiercely. 'I too had thought of having more sons, *mi amada*, and I would still like to have them with you. But because I wish to keep you with me for the rest of my days and love you as I never believed I could love until you came into my life.'

'Yet you said goodbye to me and seemed—so distant.' She remembered his formal farewell to her on the pier, what now seemed like hours ago. 'Why, Tonio?'

He held her close, his hands moving in slow persuasive strokes over her body, and she had to believe he loved her or she would have died. 'Because you seemed so anxious to leave, *enamorada*. When Madre told me that you wished to speak with me I had no idea what it was that you had to say to me, I did not care so very much. I had made up my mind that whatever you thought was my reason for wishing to marry you, I would tell you how much I loved you, and ask you. Then when you told me that you wished to return home, that you no longer wished to stay on our island, I was stunned. Too stunned to even think clearly.'

'Oh, Tonio!'

'I believed I had been what you call put firmly in my place, and I saw no hope for me.'

'But you came after me, just the same,' she murmured.

He smiled, a slow and slightly rueful smile that was infinitely endearing, so that she tiptoed and kissed his lips. 'It is a long time since I have been berated for a fool,' Antonio confessed. 'When I returned to the house, Madre fully expected you would return with me, and she told me what a fool I was to have let you go when you were so unhappy about leaving. I could doubt Andrés' word, but not Madre's, and I wished so much to believe you loved me, *mi pichon*, that I raced my horse as fiercely and cruelly as Andrés ever did back to the pier. The long boat was the only way I could catch up with you, and I borrowed it without a qualm while the man was ashore.'

Francesca looked up at him with gleaming green eyes, laughter quivering softly on her mouth. 'You mean you stole a boat to come after me?' she asked, and laughed. 'Oh, Tonio!' Hugging as close as she could to him, she buried her face against the softness of his shirt, turning her lips to the lowest point of a vee of tanned skin. 'Oh, my darling, I love you so much, I thought I'd die when I left you!'

'You will marry me?' She somehow managed to nod agreement. 'But you will keep your half of Tradaro's,'

Antonio insisted, and she raised her face to tell him that she
would quite willingly part with it, but he kissed her so long
and so fiercely that she almost forgot what she had been
going to say. 'Does it matter?' he asked, when he raised his
head eventually. 'It will belong to our sons, *mi amada*, will
it not?'

A little anxiously she regarded him for a moment. 'Not
to Andrés?'

Antonio shook his head. 'Andrés has what he wants,' he
told her with the familiar firmness she knew would brook
no argument. 'And now that I have you, my love, so have
I!'

He gathered her into his arms again and it was some time
before Francesca became aware of voices, shouting and
calling, and noticed how close they had drifted to the
freighter anchored offshore of Trader's Cay. She looked up
at Antonio and shivered at the dark glow of passion she saw
in his eyes.

'Shouldn't we take the man his boat back?' she ventured
huskily, but Antonio did not even bother to turn his head.

'A moment more, my love,' he murmured, and pressed
her close to the irresistible warmth of him. 'Just a moment
more, Francesca.'

It was a moment that would be repeated a million times
over for all the rest of their lives, Francesca thought
contentedly, and smiled as she lifted her mouth for his kiss.

Harlequin Romances

The books that let you escape
into the wonderful world of romance!
Trips to exotic places...interesting
plots...meeting memorable people...
the excitement of love....These are
integral parts of Harlequin Romances –
the heartwarming novels read by
women everywhere.

Many early issues are now available.
Choose from this great selection!

Choose from this list of Harlequin Romance editions.*

*Some of these book were originally published under different titles.

Relive a great love story...
Harlequin Romances 1980
Complete and mail this coupon today!

Harlequin Reader Service

In U.S.A.
MPO Box 707
Niagara Falls, N.Y. 14302

In Canada
649 Ontario St.
Stratford, Ontario, N5A 6W2

Please send me the following Harlequin Romance novels. I am enclosing my check or money order for $1.25 for each novel ordered, plus 59¢ to cover postage and handling.

☐ 422	☐ 509	☐ 636	☐ 729	☐ 810	☐ 902
☐ 434	☐ 517	☐ 673	☐ 737	☐ 815	☐ 903
☐ 459	☐ 535	☐ 683	☐ 746	☐ 838	☐ 909
☐ 481	☐ 559	☐ 684	☐ 748	☐ 872	☐ 920
☐ 492	☐ 583	☐ 713	☐ 798	☐ 878	☐ 927
☐ 508	☐ 634	☐ 714	☐ 799	☐ 888	☐ 941

Number of novels checked @ $1.25 each = $_____

N.Y. State residents add appropriate sales tax $_____

Postage and handling $_____ .59

TOTAL $_____

I enclose _____
(Please send check or money order. We cannot be responsible for cash sent through the mail.)

Prices subject to change without notice.

NAME _____
(Please Print)

ADDRESS _____

CITY _____

STATE/PROV. _____

ZIP/POSTAL CODE _____

Offer expires March 31, 1981

012563371